family
secrets

BRIAN KEANEY

family secrets

 ORCHARD BOOKS

ORCHARD BOOKS
96 Leonard Street, London EC2A 4XD
Orchard Books Australia
14 Mars Road, Lane Cove, NSW 2066
First published in Great Britain in 1997
First paperback publication 1997
This edition published in 2000
Text © Brian Keaney 1997
A CIP catalogue record for this book is available from the British Library.
ISBN 1 84121 530 9
1 3 5 7 9 10 8 6 4 2
Printed in Great Britain

Chapter One

IT WAS the mail that woke Kate, clattering through the letter box and landing with a soft thump on the doormat. It took a moment before she remembered what day it was, then a warm glow of satisfaction began to spread right through her. It was the first day of the summer holidays. She could do anything she wanted. She could stay in bed for as long as she liked. She could get up and go swimming, shopping, or just lounge about half dressed all day, watching TV and eating bowls of cornflakes and pieces of toast. She wriggled a little further under the duvet and began sinking back into sleep.

A few minutes later there was a knock on her bedroom door. "I've brought you some tea," Anne's voice said.

"Thanks," Kate mumbled, still only partly awake.

Her mother came into the room and put two mugs of tea down on the little cabinet beside Kate's bed. Then she sat down on the bed herself. Kate realised, with a vague feeling of annoyance, that she wasn't going to be allowed to go back to sleep.

"There's a letter for you," Anne said.

"For me?" Kate propped herself up in bed, blinking sleepily. She never got letters, probably because she never wrote any.

Anne offered her one of the two envelopes she held in her hand. It was from one of her friends, Kate could tell that without even opening it. Whoever had sent it had drawn a pattern in flowers on the back. No adult would do that. She sat up and took the envelope.

She held it in her hand for a long time, looking at it, trying to decide who it was from, but there was no clue. The writing could have been by any of her friends. She tore open the envelope, took out the letter and read:

Dear Friend,

This is a love chain. It is a game of romance since 1817. You must copy this word for word seven times (by hand) and give it to seven different people (not boys) within four days. On the fourth day drink a glass of milk and say a boy's name five times and after some days a boy will ask you out or tell you he loves you.

This is not a joke. It has worked. If you break this chain it will bring bad luck on your romance forever!!!
Good luck!

It wasn't signed.

"This is so ridiculous!" Kate said, grinning. She

wondered which of her friends could possibly have been silly enough to send it to her. She considered them in turn: Laura? No, not Laura. She was far too sensible for something like this. Emma? Perhaps. Emma was always going on about boys but she would have told Kate first. She could never keep anything secret. Lucy? Maybe. Or maybe it was just someone in her class whom she didn't know particularly well. After all you had to send it to – how many? Seven other people. That was quite a tall order. Well she certainly wasn't going to do it, anyway. Copy it out seven times. What a waste of time! Kate read it again and laughed out loud. "Why do you have to drink a glass of milk?" she said.

She looked at Anne and opened her mouth to begin telling her about the ridiculous letter, then stopped. Her mother hadn't been listening. She was reading intently the letter which had been addressed to her and frowning. She was unaware that Kate was watching her. She seemed to be reading very slowly or perhaps she was reading the same lines over and over again. As Kate watched her, her top teeth came down over her bottom lip and held it there. That was a danger sign. When Anne bit her lip, there was trouble ahead. "What's the matter?" Kate asked.

Anne looked up from the letter. There was a moment when she looked at Kate as if she didn't recognise her. Then she pulled herself together. "Nothing," she said. She folded the letter, stuffed it

3

back into its envelope and put it in the pocket of her jeans. "What are you going to do today?" she asked.

Kate knew there was no point in asking again. Anne never told you anything unless she wanted to.

"I don't know," Kate said. "I thought I'd see what the others are doing first."

"Do you want to help in the café at all?"

"Not this week, if that's all right."

"Of course it's all right," Anne said. She picked up her mug of tea and gulped it down. "I'd better get going then," she said.

The flat that Anne and Kate lived in was above Anne's café, The Hideaway. It was more of a little restaurant, really. It was open in the evenings as well and sometimes catered for parties from the offices near by. Ever since Kate could remember, they had lived above the café and, six days a week, Anne had got up early in the morning, gone downstairs and opened up. Soon the smell of coffee, toast, croissants, frying eggs and sausages would fill the flat, but Kate had grown used to that. Every holiday since she was ten years old she had spent some time helping her mother and in return Anne had increased her pocket money. It wasn't a job, Anne explained. She only needed to do it when she wanted to.

Her friends like Laura, whose father was a barrister, and Lucy, whose parents were both teachers, got plenty of pocket money without doing any extra work, but

Kate didn't really mind. There had only ever been Anne and herself and they looked after each other.

"I wasn't born for riches," Anne said once, when Kate suggested they should do the Lottery every week. "I was born for hard work." But she said it with a smile.

When Anne was ten years old, she once told Kate, she had got up every morning to help her mother milk the cows. She didn't often talk about her childhood in Ireland. It was a rare moment of intimacy. Anne had been catering for an office party one evening. Marian, her right-hand woman, had phoned in to say she was sick. So Kate had offered to help out. The party had stayed much later than Anne had expected. Several of them had been drunk and noisy. Afterwards, as Anne had tried, gently, to steer him towards the door, one of the men had put his arm round her. Kate had swelled with anger when she saw this. But Anne had firmly detached the man's hand. "That's enough of that, thank you," she had said.

"Enough of what, me darlin'?" said the man, making a clumsy attempt to imitate Anne's accent. He looked as if he was going to try to kiss her but one of his colleagues grabbed hold of him and pulled him away. "Come on, Nigel," he said. "He's just a bit drunk," he told Anne.

"I'd never have guessed," Anne said.

When they were all gone, Anne and Kate cleared

the plates away. "What a disgusting creep that man was!" Kate said.

"I shouldn't have let you stay up so late," Anne replied.

She meant, Kate realised, that she didn't want her daughter to see sights like that. "I don't mind," Kate had told her. "Anyway someone had to help."

"Thank you," Anne said.

"I like helping," Kate told her.

"Do you?"

"I like being useful."

That was when Anne had told her about milking the cows. She laughed when she said it. "I used to love it," she said. "Milking the big smelly old cows."

"Do you ever wish you still lived there?" Kate asked.

Anne shook her head. "Not one little bit," she said. She stacked the plates in the dishwasher. "Leave those," she told Kate, "and go to bed. I'll do the rest." That was what it was like with Anne. Sometimes she volunteered information but if you tried to find out anything by asking, she just closed up.

After Anne had left, Kate tried again to go back to sleep, but it was no good now. She couldn't get the image out of her mind of her mother reading the letter so intently and worrying at her lower lip with her teeth. She decided that she might as well get up and see what was going on.

Watching TV all day had seemed like a good idea, but as soon as she turned the set on, Kate remembered how awful the programmes were in the holidays. It was all cartoons for little kids. She switched off, picked up the telephone and rang Laura's number. She got the ansaphone. "Hello," said Laura's father in his voice which always sounded faintly irritated, "I'm afraid neither Penny nor John can come to the phone right now, but if you would like to leave a message after the tone, we will get back to you as soon as possible."

That was typical of Laura's parents. Anne's ansaphone messages always included Kate. "Hi," she would begin breezily, "you're out of luck, I'm afraid," or something like that. Then she would always add "if you want to leave a message for Anne or Kate, please go ahead." That wasn't Laura's father's style. He always assumed that he was the most important person, followed by his wife. Laura didn't even count. Whenever she phoned Kate up she would always end in a hurry saying something like, "I've got to go now, my dad wants to use the phone."

"It's me, Kate," she told Laura's ansaphone. "I'm just phoning up to see if you're doing anything." Then she put the receiver down and dialled Lucy's number. Her mother answered. "Oh hello, Kate," she said. "I'm afraid you've just missed Lucy. She's gone swimming."

"Oh right."

"I'll tell her you rang."

7

"Thanks." Kate put the phone down. That must be where Laura was as well. She and Lucy had got up early and gone swimming without telling anyone else. Kate rang Emma's number. Emma's little brother answered. "Who is it?" he demanded.

"It's Kate," she told him.

"Kate who?" He was always like this on the phone, demanding proof of identity, even though he knew perfectly well who she was.

"Emma's friend, Kate," she told him. "Can I speak to her?"

"She's gone swimming," he said. Then he put down the phone.

Kate felt a stab of disappointment. So they had all gone and left her out. They hadn't done that to her for ages now, but it wasn't the first time. She didn't know why it had happened. She hadn't argued with any of them. It was just a sort of meanness that came over them from time to time. They decided to leave her out of things. She would suddenly find that they didn't want to talk to her in the playground. There would be no explanation. They would just be huddled together, excluding her, saying things about her. Then one day they would have forgotten all about it. Kate sighed at the thought of it. She wanted to cry. It was the first day of the summer holidays and it was all going wrong.

It didn't get any better, either. At eleven o'clock she was eating toast and watching a discussion programme about twins. The studio was full of sets of twins, some of them identical, some of them not alike at all, but they all seemed to be agreed about how great it was to be a twin. "You always have a friend," one of them said and all the others clapped.

It only made Kate feel worse. If you had asked her, Kate would not have described herself as a lonely person. Once she had to write an essay for school about solitude and she had written: "Everybody has to learn to depend upon themselves because ultimately we all have to make our own decisions." The teacher had put a tick next to this sentence and written "Good". But it wasn't really her own thought. It was what Anne was always saying. Anne was big on independence. That was why she didn't freak out when the drunk put his arm around her in the café. "I have learned how to handle myself," she told Kate, "and so must you." That was on one of the previous occasions when Laura, Emma and Lucy had decided to leave her out of things. "They'll come round," Anne had predicted. "In the meantime depend upon yourself." Anne had been right, of course. They had come round, but it had been hard waiting for them, standing around in the playground by herself, eating her lunch without anyone to talk to. She still didn't know what it had all been about, either that time or this. Some people just seemed to need to behave like that, as far as she could see.

She turned off the programme about twins and

picked up a magazine. She was reading an article entitled 'What Do Boys Really Want?' when she heard the key turning in the door of the flat. It was Anne. She put her head around the doorway of the living room. "I thought you might have gone out," she said.

"No," Kate said. She didn't feel like explaining all about the swimming.

"I've got a few phone calls to make," Anne said. "I'll be in my office."

Anne's 'office' was where she went when she had to sort out her accounts, write polite letters to the bank or call up catering suppliers, but she generally set aside Thursday afternoons for this, not Monday mornings. Kate had a feeling that this was something unusual, something to do with the letter she had received that morning, perhaps.

"Is everything all right, Mum?" she asked.

"Right as rain," Anne called back, disappearing into the office and closing the door behind her.

Kate couldn't concentrate on her magazine. She knew Anne better than anyone else on the planet and she knew that there was something wrong. You could tell just from the way she spoke, from the tightness of the lines around her mouth. Kate had seen this before when the café had been going through difficult times, when the bank had threatened to call in the overdraft, but that was all in the past now. As far as she knew, the café had been doing well for a long time. Nowadays, when there were things to buy for school or letters home about foreign trips, Anne didn't clench her fists and look as if she had chewed on a lemon, she just wrote a cheque and handed it over. But maybe it had just been a temporary phase, maybe it would be back to making do with old clothes and saying no to school trips.

When Anne emerged, half an hour later, she didn't go back down to the café. Instead she came into the living room and sat on the sofa opposite Kate. Kate put down her magazine and waited for whatever it was that was coming.

"I've had some bad news, Kate," Anne began.

"Was it in the letter this morning?"

"Yes."

"What's happened?"

"My mother's had a stroke."

This was not what Kate had expected at all.

"She's in hospital. They don't know whether she'll recover or not."

Anne hadn't spoken about her mother in years and years. When Kate was about six years old, she had come back from school one day and asked, "Have I got a grandma and grandpa?" and Anne had explained to her that her grandpa was dead and her grandma lived in Ireland.

"Can we go and see her?" six-year-old Kate had asked.

"She doesn't want to see us," Anne had replied.

Kate could remember the occasion clearly, the terrible sense of hurt that seemed to swallow her up.

"Why doesn't she want to?" she had asked in a very little voice.

"Because she doesn't," was all that Anne had said.

Another time, Anne had explained a little more. They were sitting on the same sofa that Anne was sitting on now. Kate must have been about eight years old. They had been watching television. It was a children's programme and the girl in it had just been given a birthday present by her grandma. It was a dress and it was very pretty with silk ribbons, only that wasn't what she wanted. What she wanted was a skateboard and she was trying to explain this to her grandmother without hurting her feelings. After the programme had finished Kate had wanted to ask Anne about her grandmother but had said nothing. It was hard to ask Anne about something that she didn't want to tell you about. She put up a sort of invisible barrier, like a force-field that prevented you from speaking. But finally Kate had managed to pluck up the courage to ask, "Why doesn't my grandma like me?"

"It isn't that she doesn't like you," Anne said.

"But you said she didn't want to see me."

Anne sighed. "It's not you she doesn't want to see," she explained. "It's me."

"Why?"

"She disapproves of me."

"But why?"

"It's because I'm not married," Anne said.

Kate looked at her in amazement. "But what's that got to do with anything?" she demanded.

Anne shrugged. "I don't know," she said.

Kate was baffled. Some children lived with fathers and mothers, others with just one parent, some with step-parents and some were adopted. That was one of the first things that Anne had explained to her and she had found out that it was true when she went to school and met other children. Her friend Emma lived with her mother and step-father; several other children in her class at primary school lived with just one parent.

"She's a very traditional person," Anne explained.

"What does that mean?"

"It means that she thinks people should only have children if they are married," Anne said.

"That's the reason why she doesn't want to see us?" Kate asked. It seemed so ridiculous.

"That's the reason," Anne agreed.

"But that's stupid."

"People are stupid sometimes."

Since that time, Anne had hardly mentioned her mother and Kate had known better than to ask her. She was part of Anne's past, not Kate's. That was how it had always been, until now.

"So what's going to happen?" Kate asked.

"I'm going to have to go over there," Anne said.

"To Ireland?"

"Yes."

"What about me?"

"You'll have to come too, naturally."

"For how long?"

"I don't know."

Kate was silent. A mixture of feelings was welling up inside her.

"We can get a flight to Dublin tomorrow morning at ten o'clock. Then we'll have to get a train to the west, that's if there still is one. I need to get through to the railway people to find out. It's a long train journey I'm afraid."

It was all worked out already, most of it anyway. That was so typical of Anne: she never consulted Kate, never asked for her opinion, just went ahead and made the arrangements and expected Kate to fall into line.

"I don't want to go," Kate said, at last.

"I know you don't," Anne said. "But what else can we do?"

"I could stay here," Kate suggested.

"You're only thirteen years old."

"So? I'd be perfectly all right."

"I'm sure you would, Kate, but it's out of the question."

"Why?"

"Because I'd be failing in my duty as a mother."

"You wouldn't. I can look after myself."

"Other people wouldn't see it that way. Anyway, it's probably against the law. You'll have to come with me. Unless ..."

"Unless what?" Kate demanded eagerly.

"Unless you could stay with one of your friends," Anne said. "I don't suppose ..." She looked at Kate expectantly.

Kate shook her head. "I'll come," she said.

"It'll be a change," Anne suggested.

A change! A visit to a strange country to see an old woman who didn't want to see you. Kate felt angry at the thought. She wanted to say, "Why do we have to worry about her anyway? She's never worried about us." But she didn't. Instead she asked, "How long will we have to stay?"

"I don't know. It depends on how things turn out." Anne leant forward and kissed Kate on the cheek. "I've got to make some more phone calls," she said. She got up and went back into the office.

That was it then. Kate sat there, her magazine still open on her lap. The summer holidays had been hijacked and there was not even time to discuss it.

Half an hour later Anne re-emerged from her office. "We can get the one o'clock train," she said. "We can get a cab from Dublin airport to Connolly Station." She was talking to herself, really. Kate had seen her like this before when the café had been going through its bad

15

patch. It was her crisis mode. "You need to get packed," she said, as if she had suddenly remembered that she was coming too. "I'll get the bags down from on top of the wardrobe."

"I can get them." Kate was nearly as tall as her mother but this had somehow failed to register with Anne, who often still acted as if Kate was a little girl. Kate went into her bedroom and took down the big holdall that she used whenever they went on holiday. "How much stuff should I take?" she called out.

"Take enough for a fortnight."

"A fortnight!"

"Just to be on the safe side."

Kate opened the drawers of the chest that contained her clothes. This was getting worse and worse. At first it was just a few days. Now they could be gone for a whole fortnight.

"Pack warm clothes," Anne said, putting her head around the bedroom door.

"But it's boiling," Kate protested. It was true. For the last few weeks it had just got hotter and hotter.

"You can't rely on the weather in Ireland," Anne told her, coming into the room. "You'd better bring a coat as well."

"A coat!"

"Just in case. It's bound to rain for part of the time."

"But it's the end of July."

"Have you got any wellingtons?" Anne asked, ignoring Kate's protest.

"Wellingtons!"

"I hope you're not going to stand there repeating every word I say," Anne said.

"I won't need wellingtons, surely?"

"You might."

"Well I haven't got any."

"What about those ones I bought you when you went on that school trip to Devon?"

Kate sighed. "Mum, that was a year ago," she said. "They're miles too small."

"We'll just have to hope for the best then," Anne said. She went out of the bedroom.

Chapter Two

THEY WENT by tube to the airport the next morning. It was hot and crowded and the journey seemed to go on for ever. Kate's bag was heavy and she had trouble managing it. Whatever way she tried to carry it, the bag kept getting in the way and hitting people. When they reached the airport, they had to queue to check in and then, after they had been given their boarding cards and gone through into the departure lounge, they sat on uncomfortable seats until they were allowed to board the plane.

The air hostess stood just inside the plane smiling at everyone who came on board. She gave Kate a special smile and said, "Hello there." She was trying to be nice, of course – Kate realised that. But there was something about her manner that suggested she thought Kate was about six years old.

Kate had always assumed that when she became a teenager she would begin to have a bit of freedom and to live her own life. She had imagined that people would treat her more or less like an adult. In fact it seemed to be turning out quite the opposite.

After the plane had taken off, the air hostess came over to Kate and handed her a plastic bag. "With the compliments of the airline," she said. Kate looked at the bag. It had *Young Fliers Club* written on the front.

The bag contained a colouring book and colouring pencils, a plane-spotter's guide and a game of portable magnetic chequers. "Thank you," Kate said.

"What is it?" Anne asked, when the hostess had gone away.

Kate showed her.

"She meant well," Anne said.

"I know," Kate replied, but that didn't make it any better. She watched as the hostess carried on down the plane and gave out two more bags to kids who looked scarcely old enough to have started primary school.

The flight lasted just over an hour and there was nothing to see, just clouds out of the window and the back of the seat in front. A lot of the time seemed to be taken up with a determined attempt by the cabin crew to sell them duty-free drinks and perfume. After they had landed, Kate and Anne disembarked and went to the baggage hall to collect their luggage which was delivered on a conveyer belt from somewhere in the depths of the airport. Their bags took ever such a long time to arrive and Kate was beginning to wonder whether they might have got lost. Almost everyone else seemed to have collected theirs. Then at last the bags appeared, side by side on the conveyer belt. "Like me and Anne," Kate thought to herself.

They picked up their luggage and walked through the crowd of people waiting in the arrivals hall.

"What time is the train?" Kate asked.

"One o'clock," Anne told her.

"One o'clock!" Kate exclaimed. "There must be one before that."

"There are only three a day," Anne told her, "one in the morning, one in the afternoon and one in the evening."

"Don't people get fed up waiting?"

"There aren't many people going where we're going," Anne said. "It's a very thinly populated part of the world."

They took a cab to the station, left their bags in the left-luggage office and went to look around the city.

They had lunch in a very pretty restaurant, called Bewleys. The walls were covered with old oak panelling, the floor was a mosaic of tiny stones and the waitresses were all wearing old-fashioned costumes. "This is where I used to come when I was a girl," Anne said. "Once or twice a year we used to come down to Dublin and we always came straight here from the station."

"Is that why you started a café of your own?" Kate asked.

"Not really. Waitressing was just the first job I got when I came to England, and I stuck to it. I had some money put away, from when my father died, so in time I was able to start up in business myself."

"I prefer your café to this one," said Kate.

Anne laughed. "That's very loyal," she said. "But I think you're a wee bit biased."

After they had killed as much time as was possible, they walked back to the station, collected their bags and boarded the train. They had to wait for another twenty minutes before it left.

"I still can't believe there are only three trains a day," Kate said. "This part of the journey is taking so long."

"Rule number one in Ireland," Anne told her. "No one is in a hurry."

At last the train pulled slowly out of Dublin and they watched as the little houses that were clustered closely together in the centre of the city grew further and further apart. "Has Ireland changed much?" Kate asked her mother. "Since you left, I mean?"

Anne thought about the question. "In some ways it's changed a lot," she said. "Dublin is much busier than it was. That's how it looks to me, anyway. The airport's been smartened up. But I think that's all on the surface. Underneath I don't think it's changed at all."

A ticket collector came past and asked them for

their tickets. He was an old man with a red face.

"Now," he said as he clipped the tickets and handed them back, "are you on holiday?"

"Not really," Anne said.

"Going home then?" He spoke with an extremely strong accent.

"In a way."

"Let's hope the weather picks up for you," he said and began to move off.

"Is there a buffet on the train?" Kate said.

The ticket collector looked puzzled. "A what?" he asked.

"Somewhere you can get something to eat and drink," Kate explained.

"There is of course. Rear of the train. Third car along." He smiled at Anne. "I have trouble with the accent," he said with a wink.

Kate waited until the ticket collector had moved further up the train.

"What did he mean by that?" she demanded.

"He meant that he couldn't understand your accent," Anne told her.

"What a cheek!" Kate thought to herself. After all, he was the one with the accent.

The train trundled along at a steady pace, its old-fashioned carriages rattling over the lines in a rhythm that never stopped. It reminded Kate of someone playing a drum kit. Rain, which had begun as startled spots on the train windows, was now running down the glass relentlessly. She stared out at the landscape in wonder. It was so different. At least Dublin had looked a bit like London, only smaller, but very soon the city had been left behind for green fields with huge round bundles of hay lying in the middle of them like swiss rolls. In some places the corn had not been cut and stood tall in the fields, criss-crossed by paths that looked like the partings in an enormous head of hair.

The further they travelled the wilder the countryside became. Corn fields gave way to stony ground with sheep dotted all about. The few houses that they passed were perched oddly on the hillsides between clumps of trees and straggling hedges. Everywhere, too, there was water: ditches, ponds and flooded land.

"It must have been raining here for days," Kate said.

"Looks like it," her mother replied.

Just looking out of the window you could tell that this land was used to rain. Everything was so green; that was the first thing you noticed. The second thing was that there were very few people. After the first station there hadn't been another stop for an hour. And only three people had boarded the train there. There was a long wait while they got on board, saying goodbye to the people who waved them off. Then a green flag was waved and the train pulled away. On the way out of the station a woman and a baby stood on a bridge and waved as the train passed underneath. Kate pointed them out to her mother.

"I remember when I used to get excited at the sight of a train," Anne said. "It was a big thing to a little girl."

"I suppose people just get used to it," Kate said.

"I suppose they do," Anne said. "There's a saying, 'It's better to travel than to arrive.' Did you ever hear that?"

"No. What does it mean?"

"It means that the experience of travelling somewhere is more important than actually getting there."

Kate thought about this. She didn't think that she agreed. She could never understand it when people said they like travelling. It was what models always said when they were interviewed. But Kate was never going to be a model. She knew that. She wasn't tall enough or pretty enough. Laura had told her.

It was shortly after she had joined secondary school and Kate had not known very many other girls there. Laura had seemed so sophisticated with her long blonde hair that swished when she turned her head, and Kate had badly wanted to be friends with her. They were standing in a group in the playground talking when Laura had announced that she wanted to be a model.

"So do I," Kate had said immediately. She had no idea why she said it since the idea of being a model had never even occurred to her before.

Laura turned and looked at her with her cold blue eyes. "You couldn't be a model," she said. "You're not tall enough."

"I'm still growing," Kate replied.

"I've seen your mother," Laura said scornfully. "She's not tall. Anyway, you're not pretty enough."

Kate had made no reply to this. It seemed impossible to argue with. Up until then she had never really given a thought to whether she was pretty or not. Now she knew for certain. She was not. Not pretty enough anyway.

Shortly after that, Laura had decided that she did not wish to be a model after all; she was going to be a politician instead. Ever since that time, travelling had always seemed like an empty and trivial ambition to Kate. She had enjoyed going to France with Anne the year before last, and she had enjoyed the school trips she had been on. But it was *being* somewhere that she liked, not travelling. The travelling was just boring.

Kate had brought a small travel bag as well as her big holdall. She stood up and took it down from the luggage rack. She opened it and brought out a writing pad, biro and her address book. Then she put the bag back and sat down. Out of her pocket she took the chain letter she had received the morning before.

"What are you doing?" Anne asked as Kate spread out the letter in front of her.

"I'm just writing to a friend," Kate said.

Kate wasn't sure exactly when she had made up her mind to take part in the love chain. She had picked up the letter after she had packed her clothes and re-read it. Then she had put her address book and a writing pad in the travel bag, just in case.

Now that there seemed nothing else particularly worth doing on the journey, she decided that she might as well follow the instructions. After all, what had she got to lose?

An hour later, Kate's hand was aching slightly but she was finishing the last letter as they stopped at a station called Carrick. It was a pretty station with old-fashioned buildings. The name was written in flowers that grew in the bank alongside the platform. A handful of passengers got on and then the train pulled away. The guard came back again.

"You're in the West, now," he told them. He went off up the train collecting the tickets of any new passengers.

Carrick was left behind in moments. On either side now were green fields divided up in a higgledy-piggledy fashion by stone walls and hedges. Huge rocks lay scattered all over them as if a giant people had passed through the place centuries ago, littering it with stones. The sky began to grow dark and stormy and all the countryside that they passed through seemed empty. Occasionally Kate glimpsed tumbledown stone cottages, their white walls looming like ghosts under the darkening sky.

"What is a stroke, exactly?" Kate asked her mother. She had finished the letters and the envelopes and there was nothing else to do except think.

"It's a blood clot," Anne said. "The flow of blood to the brain is interrupted and the brain can be damaged as a result."

"But why is it called a stroke?" Kate asked. There seemed to be no connection between the illness and its name.

"To tell you the truth, I don't know," Anne said. "I think it might be because in the old days people thought it meant you were struck down by God, or something."

"How weird!" Kate said.

"I expect people thought it was a punishment," Anne went on. "For something you had done wrong."

"I'm glad I wasn't alive in those days," Kate said.

The train travelled relentlessly onward. Kate looked out of the window less often now. She was tired of looking out, tired of the whole long journey that had begun with the tube ride to the airport that morning.

"How long have we been on this train?" Kate asked.

"Fifteen minutes later than the last time you asked," her mother told her. "Three hours and fifteen minutes."

27

"Another half hour," Kate said. She knew she was whining but she couldn't help herself.

"Oh, Kate, do you have to go on about it?" her mother said. "Why don't you read or something?"

"I didn't bring a book," Kate said.

"Here, read this," Anne said. She handed Kate a copy of her newspaper.

"It's boring," Kate complained.

"Read it," she ordered. "You might learn something."

Kate skimmed through the pages but found nothing to interest her. She folded it up again. "What will it be like?" she asked. "I mean, really?"

"I don't know, Kate."

"Are you worried?"

"A bit."

"I wish we didn't have to go."

"So do I. But there's no point in going on about it."

Kate looked mournfully out of the window.

"It won't be long now," Anne said.

Chapter Three

KATE AND Anne were the only passengers to disembark at the tiny ramshackle station of Cruachan. They stood on the platform holding their bags and looking around them as the train pulled away down the line.

"What now?" Kate asked. She suddenly felt as if they were lost. Since waking up that morning they had been striving to get here, covering mile after mile by tube and plane and train. Now here they were, two forlorn figures standing on a windswept platform in the middle of nowhere.

"I thought there would be someone to meet us," Anne said. "Come on, let's have a look for him." She began to walk down the platform towards the exit.

"Who are we looking for?" Kate asked.

"Aidan. He's a neighbour of my mother's. I expect he'll be along in a minute."

They went past the booking office, which was closed and shuttered, and out on to a forecourt that was completely deserted. A driveway led from the forecourt down to the main road, which curled away into the distance between steeply rising hills.

"Where's the town?" Kate asked.

"The station is about a mile outside the town," Anne told her. She pointed to the empty road.

As they watched, a car came into sight, its engine labouring noisily. There was a crunch of gears as it turned into the station driveway.

"That'll be Aidan," Anne said. "He always was a terrible driver."

The car that pulled up in front of them was battered and mud-stained and so was the driver. He got out and came over to them. He stood looking at Anne for a moment and then he said, "Anne Gallagher you haven't changed one bit." He seized her arm and began pumping it up and down.

Anne laughed. "Will you let go of my arm before you break it, Aidan," she said.

It seemed to Kate that her mother's accent had become noticeably more Irish.

Aidan turned to her. "Is this Kathleen?" he asked. He pronounced it "Kat-leen".

"Kate," she told him.

"You're very welcome to Ireland, Kate," he said. He took her hand in his, but instead of pumping it up and down as he had done Anne's, he only squeezed it gently. His hand was massive and felt as if it wasn't covered with skin at all but with some much tougher substance like leather.

"Let's get in out of the wind," Aidan said, letting go of her hand. He picked up their bags as if they were no weight at all, strolled over to the car, opened the boot and put them in. Then Anne got into the front passenger seat and Kate got into the back of the car.

The car had a strange smell, Kate decided, a sort of earthy, outdoors smell, not altogether unpleasant, but not what you might expect either. The engine grumbled into life again when Aidan turned the key in the ignition and, with a crunching of the gears, they swung away from the kerb, down the driveway, towards the road that wound between the hills.

As he drove, Aidan told them that Anne's mother was still in hospital, that she had recovered consciousness but that she had not spoken yet. He said that he and his wife, Maureen, had been looking after the house. "We have it all ready for you," he said.

"How's everybody in Cruachan?" Anne asked him.

"They're all grand, of course," Aidan said. "They were all asking after you, when I said I'd written."

"Who were?"

"Everyone. They haven't forgotten you around here, you know."

He carried on talking, telling Anne about people she had known when she was a girl. Their names meant nothing to Kate and the talk drifted over her head.

Little by little she found herself slipping into dreams about colouring books and swimming pools that seemed to make perfect sense and yet made no sense at all. Suddenly the car stopped. "What's the matter?" she demanded.

Anne's voice came reassuringly from the front of the car. "Nothing's the matter."

"Then why have we stopped?"

"Because we've arrived."

Kate sat up and shivered. She looked out of the window. They were parked in front of a house. It was not at all as she had expected it. She had imagined a little thatched cottage with whitewashed walls, but this was a tall building with a slate roof which shone with the rain that was just beginning to fall out of the late afternoon sky. She got out of the car and went and stood beside Anne who was staring at the house. Her mother's eyes, Kate realised, were brimming with tears.

Kate put her arm around her mother. "Are you sad?" she asked.

Anne nodded but she didn't speak.

Aidan got out of the car and went round to the boot to take the bags out. Then he led the way inside. They went through the back door and into the kitchen. It was a big room, but it was dominated by a huge old-fashioned stove at one end. All kinds of pots and pans and kitchen utensils were hanging by hooks from the ceiling above it.

"I'll get the stove lit," Aidan said, putting down the bags, "and then it'll look a bit more cheerful."

Anne stood looking round at the room, taking in every detail.

Aidan opened the door of the stove, struck a match, and lit the papers which were screwed up beneath wood and something that looked like coal, but was not coal.

"What is that stuff?" Kate asked him.

"This?" He took a piece out and handed it to Kate. It was brown, hard and crumbly, a bit like a fossilised piece of cake. "It's turf," he told her.

"I thought turf was grass."

"It is, but this is what we call turf around here."

"Where does it come from?"

"Up in the bog beyond. It's dug out of the ground."

Kate watched as the flames licked around the pieces of turf, which quickly began to burn. Aidan shut the door of the stove. "That's that taken care of," he said. "Now I think it's time for a cup of tea."

"I'll make that," Anne said. They were the first words she had spoken since getting out of the car, and she spoke them like someone coming out of a trance.

"You will not," Aidan told her. "Sit down there like a good girl and behave."

Kate was amazed to hear this man speaking to her mother as if she was a little girl. She expected Anne to put him in his place right away, but instead she meekly did as she was told while Aidan busied himself around the kitchen, filling the kettle, getting cups and saucers down, putting milk in to a jug.

"You'll be wanting something to eat," Aidan said. It was a statement, not a question. He went over to a cupboard and brought out a bundle wrapped in a tea-towel. He put it down in the middle of the table and unwrapped it. It looked a bit like a cake and a bit like a loaf.

"What is it?" Kate asked.

"It's a braic," Anne said. "Did Maureen bake it?" she asked Aidan.

"She did indeed. In your honour."

Aidan took a bread knife out of the drawer and began sawing away at the braic, cutting thick slices which he spread with soft yellow butter and piled up on a plate in the middle of the table. "Help yourselves," he told them.

When Aidan had first produced the braic, Kate had felt sure that she wasn't hungry, but as soon as she began to eat, she realised that she was famished. She ate piece after piece, washing them down with mouthfuls of hot tea. The temperature in the kitchen rose as the stove began to warm up. Kate stretched her legs out under the table and yawned. "I could go to sleep now," she said.

"Could you hold out until we've been to the hospital?" Anne said.

"Tonight?" Kate asked. The idea of getting up, going back out into the cold and driving off to the hospital seemed too much to ask after she had already come so far.

"You can stay here, if you like," Anne said.

"I'll come," Kate said. Anne wanted her company, she could tell that.

"You don't have to."

"It's all right, honest."

"Thanks, Kate."

"Well, I'll love you and leave you," Aidan said. "Oh I nearly forgot." He put his hand in his pocket and drew out a bunch of keys. "The keys to your mother's car. It's in the garage."

"Thanks." Anne took the keys from him.

Aidan opened the door to go. Then he paused. "Don't expect too much, at the hospital I mean," he said. "Your mother's very ill."

"I won't," Anne said. "And thanks, Aidan."

After he had gone, Kate said, "How old is he?"

Anne shrugged. "A few years older than me," she said.

Kate looked hard at her mother. "He seems much older than you," she said.

"He was always like that," Anne said. "He was an old man when he was a little boy."

"Is that why you let him boss you around?"

Anne laughed. "I suppose so," she said. "It's

amazing what you put up with from your friends."

"Did you miss your friends – when you came to England, I mean?"

Anne shook her head. "I had you to look after. That was enough to keep me busy. Come on now. Let's get started before we fall asleep sitting here in the warm."

Chapter Four

KATE HATED hospitals. Just the smell of them was enough to make her start to panic. It was a smell that you got nowhere else, a mixture of clean, chemical fragrances and an underlying odour of sickness. Kate had only been in hospital once, when she was eight. She had fallen out of a tree in Lucy's garden. She had tumbled head first and cut her forehead on a brick.

Lucy's mother had driven her to the local casualty department where she had received three stitches just above her eyebrow. The nurse had asked her how she had got the cut and Kate had explained. The nurse had frowned. "Little girls shouldn't go climbing trees, should they?" she said to Kate. It was a stupid thing to say and Kate had refused to answer her. She had simply looked away. The nurse had tried to be nice to her after that, but Kate wasn't interested.

Her mother had arrived a few minutes later and had put her arms around Kate, so she had forgotten about the nurse. She had been worried that she would get into trouble for getting blood all over her dress, but Anne hadn't even mentioned it. Afterwards, she was left with a small white scar just above her right eyebrow. No hairs grew on the skin of that scar, which meant that one eyebrow was different to the other. Anne told her that nobody except herself could tell the difference, but Kate was not so sure. She often sat in front of the mirror, carefully combing her eyebrows to try and make them match.

They stood inside the foyer of the hospital looking at a list of all the departments. Anne's mother was in ward C, and according to the list that was on the next floor up. They climbed the stairs and followed the signs along the corridor towards C and D wards.

"Have you ever had to go to hospital?" Kate asked.

"Only to have you," Anne told her.

"Were you frightened?"

"I was terrified."

Anne had been seventeen when Kate was born, only four years older than Kate was now. She still looked young and people often mistook them for sisters.

C ward was full of old women. They looked up at Anne and Kate with vague curiosity. It was not the official visiting time and there were no other visitors to be seen.

"Is she in this ward?" Kate asked.

"I don't know. I thought she was. I'll try and find someone to ask. You stay here."

Kate stood at the entrance to the ward, looking nervously about her. The faces of the old women depressed and even frightened Kate. It seemed to her that they were only waiting for death to come and collect them.

One woman, whose bed was next to the entrance, suddenly seemed to take notice of Kate. She beckoned with her finger. Kate looked around her in surprise, wondering if the old woman had meant somebody else, but there seemed to be no one else that she could have meant. Kate walked over to the old woman.

The old woman fixed her eyes on Kate. "I must get out of here," she said.

"Sorry?"

"I have to get out of this place."

"What do you mean?"

"I have to get home to cook the dinner for my family. They'll all be waiting for me at home. They won't know what's happened to me?" The old woman seemed completely in earnest. Her eyes were full of tears.

"But don't they know you're here?" Kate asked her.

"Of course they don't. Will you help me get out?"

"I don't know."

The woman took hold of Kate's arm. Her grip was surprisingly strong. "I have to get back and cook the dinner," she repeated. "They'll all be waiting for me. They won't know where I've got to."

"There, now, Molly," said a reassuring voice from behind Kate. She turned round to see a nurse smiling at the old woman. The nurse gently detached the old woman's hand from Kate's arm. "You know you shouldn't be getting excited."

"She said she's got to go home, to cook the dinner," Kate told the nurse. "She said her family don't know she's here."

"Now then, Molly, your family are all grown up. Wasn't your son in here only this morning with his wife?"

Molly sat back on the bed without another word. "She's just a little bit confused," the nurse told Kate. "It happens to old people sometimes."

Kate shivered. So this was what growing old meant.

"Were you looking for somebody?" the nurse asked.

"My grandmother," Kate said.

"And what's her name?"

"Gallagher," Kate said. She realised with dismay that she didn't even know her grandmother's first name. Just then Anne reappeared. "I've found out where she is," she said.

"Right then," the nurse said. "I'll get on." She smiled at them both and walked briskly away.

"She's in a little room on her own on the other side of the ward," Anne said.

She led the way and Kate followed her down the

middle of the ward. Kate glanced back at the old woman the nurse had called Molly and thought how strange and how sad that in her old age she was still worrying about the jobs she had to do when she was younger.

On the other side of the ward was a series of little rooms, each with a single bed in them. They stopped in front of one with C9 written on the door.

"Right," Anne said. She hesitated and Kate could see that this was not easy for her. Then she knocked at the door, opened it and walked in.

The woman lying on the bed was connected by tubes to bottles and instruments. She seemed very thin and fragile, as if she might break into pieces if anyone touched her. Her skin, which was the colour of parchment, was stretched across her face. Her eyes were closed. It was possible, if you looked for long enough, to see the faintest possible movement of her chest upwards and downwards, under the bedclothes, but that was the only indication that she was alive at all.

As they stood there, looking at her, another nurse came into the room behind them, wheeling a trolley. "She's not really supposed to have visitors, you know," she told them.

"I'm her daughter," Anne said. "I've come over from England."

"All right then," the nurse said, "but you won't disturb her now, will you?"

41

"No."

"That's good." She took a plastic bottle of some clear liquid from the trolley and set about exchanging it for the one which hung above the bed and from which a tube ran into Kate's grandmother's mouth.

There was only one chair beside the bed. "Sit down," Anne told Kate. "I'll go and find another chair."

Kate sat down and watched while the nurse went about her work deftly and efficiently. She wondered what it would be like to work in a place like this, dealing every day with people who were sick, some of whom would never recover. She looked at her grandmother and struggled to see Anne's face, or even her own, but she could find no resemblance at all.

Anne came back a moment later carrying a chair, which she placed beside Kate's. "We'll just stay for a little while," she said, sitting down.

The nurse went out of the room again and they sat on in the silence. It seemed a strange thing to do, just to sit there. Kate wondered what her mother was thinking.

Once, when Kate was about nine years old, one of the customers in the café had developed a crush on Anne. His name was Nick and he worked as the catering manager in one of the big hotels in the centre of London. Anne had told her this later. He had started coming into the café on Saturday mornings when Kate had been helping out, and she had seen the way he looked at her mother. Then one Saturday a huge bouquet of flowers was delivered, the biggest bunch of flowers Kate had ever seen. They were wrapped up in cellophane and pink ribbon. Nick himself had turned up shortly afterwards and had asked Anne if she would go out to the theatre with him. In her usual quietly determined way, Anne had said no. Kate had been surprised at this. She had expected her mother to say yes. Nick was very good-looking and he was well dressed, but this didn't seem to make any difference. Nick did not give up easily. Over the next few weeks he had sent more flowers and he had kept on asking her, but Anne remained completely uninterested.

"Why don't you go out with him, Mum?" Kate had asked her. She had felt disappointed on Nick's behalf. After all he was certainly trying his best.

"What would be the point?" Anne asked.

Kate could think of nothing to say in reply to this.

In the end Nick had given up. The flowers had stopped arriving and Nick had started taking breakfast somewhere else.

There had been other admirers and not all of them had fared as badly as Nick. Anne had occasionally gone out with a man and left Kate with a baby-sitter, usually Marian who managed the restaurant whenever Anne was away. But none of these brief relationships ever lasted for more than a few weeks at a time and none of Anne's admirers had impressed Kate like Nick. He had seemed almost like a character from a fairy tale with his smart suits and his flowers. For some reason the silence of that hospital room brought his face to the surface of Kate's memory, his eagerness to please and her mother's determined resistance.

Anne's chair scraped on the floor as she stood up. "Shall we go?" she said.

They retraced their steps back through the ward full of old women. Kate looked for Molly and saw her sitting up in bed looking anxiously about her. She began beckoning to Kate, as soon as she caught sight of her, but this time Kate took no notice.

Afterwards, when they were driving home through the pitch-dark of the countryside, Kate said, "Do you remember Nick, who gave you all those flowers?"

Ann laughed, grimly. "My God!" she said. "What made you think of him?"

"I don't know. I just did. Did you ever regret not going out with him?"

"Not one bit. He was as wet as water."

Now it was Kate's turn to laugh. "What does that mean?" she asked.

Anne shrugged. "I don't know," she said. "It means he was a bit hopeless."

"But he was very good-looking," Kate said.

"Was he? I didn't notice."

"You might have found that you liked him, if you'd given him a chance."

"I did like him," Anne said, "well sort of, anyway. There was nothing about him to dislike. It's just that I didn't need him."

Suddenly she braked sharply as something appeared in the headlights in front of them. Just as quickly it was gone again.

"Did you see that?" Anne asked.

"No. What was it?"

"A hare."

"Oh I wish I'd seen it."

"I expect you'll see another one. The country around here is full of them. They used to say it was good luck if a hare ran across your path."

"I thought that was black cats."

"Hares as well. At least over here it is."

They drove on in silence for a while, then Kate said, "What's Grandma's name, her first name I mean?"

"Nora."

"I don't like that name."

"Don't you?"

"It sounds old-fashioned."

"She is old-fashioned."

"Is that why she was so hard on you, about being pregnant I mean?" Kate asked.

Anne nodded. "Yes," she said. Then she added, "Only it's more than that."

"What do you mean?"

"Anne sighed. "It's so hard to explain," she said.

"Try," Kate urged her.

"The world was so different then."

"What do you mean?"

"I mean that sort of thing really mattered to people."

"But why?" Kate demanded. "It's just stupid."

"I know, Kate," Anne said, "but that's the way we were. The rules of society were very much stricter, and if you broke the rules, you had to pay."

"But was it like that in London too?" Kate asked.

Anne shook her head. "No one knew who I was in London. People are too busy to worry about what everyone else is doing. That's the great thing about cities. You can be anonymous."

"Do you think she'll recover?"

Anne shook her head. "I don't know," she said. "Perhaps I'll get a chance to talk to someone to-morrow."

By the time they got back to the old house, Kate was yawning.

They parked the car in the garage and Anne turned off the engine. The headlights went out and immediately they were plunged into total blackness. "Wow!" Kate said. "It's so dark."

They got out of the car and Kate felt her way out of the garage. Gradually her eyes became accustomed to the dark and she stood looking up at the stars while Anne locked the garage door. "I've never seen the sky like that before," Kate said. "You can see all the stars. There are millions of them."

"You should see it in the winter time, on a frosty night," Anne told her. "Here, take my hand." She reached out and took Kate's hand and led her over the drive towards the house.

"You'll sleep well tonight," she said as she opened the door.

Kate nodded. Only twenty-four hours earlier she had been packing her bag in the flat above the café. It seemed like a long time ago. Anne was right. She would sleep well and in the morning she would find out if there was anything at all for a thirteen-year-old girl to do.

Chapter Five

WHEN SHE woke up the next morning Kate had absolutely no idea where she was. She lay there with her eyes wide open, staring at the ceiling. It was not the ceiling of her own room, she knew that much. Then it all came back to her. She looked around her at the little bedroom. She had been too tired the night before to take in any of its details.

It was a small room. There was just space enough for the bed in which she was sleeping, a chest of drawers with a mirror on the top, and a little bedside table with a reading lamp placed on top of it. Above the bed was a bookshelf with a line of books on it. The room was painted blue and there were blue check curtains at the window. There was no carpet on the floor, only bare boards and a rug on the floor beside the bed with a pattern of blue and red flowers on it.

Kate reached up to the bookshelf and chose a book at random. She looked at the title on the spine: *The Turfcutter's Donkey*. She opened the book. Inside, in spidery handwriting, someone had written, "To Anne. Happy Birthday from Mummy and Daddy."

Kate realised that this must have been her mother's own bedroom. To her surprise she found tears pricking behind her eyes. "Why do I want to cry?" she wondered. It wasn't as if the room had belonged to somebody who was now dead. It had belonged to Anne whom Kate could hear even now clattering about downstairs in the kitchen. But there was something about the message in the book that was so sad. Kate could almost imagine what Anne had been like as a little girl, waking up in this bedroom on the morning of her birthday, tearing the paper off her birthday presents, opening this book and reading the message inside. She could almost see Anne's mother and father standing beside the bed, eagerly watching the expression on their daughter's face to see whether or not she liked the present. Why had it all gone so badly wrong? Kate closed the book and put it back on the shelf. She got out of bed and drew back the curtains. The sun was shining outside. She decided to get dressed.

Anne had been to a local shop and there was a choice of cornflakes or toast for breakfast. Kate chose cornflakes. They were exactly the same brand as they bought at home, but somehow they tasted different.

"Are Irish cornflakes different to English ones?" Kate asked.

"Not one bit," Anne said. "Anyway, these are made

in the UK. It says so on the box."

"Why do they taste different then?"

"Because you're thinking about it, I expect," Anne suggested. "At home you just shovel them in."

"I don't shovel!" Kate protested.

Anne raised her eyebrows. "I think I'll go into the hospital again," she announced. "You don't have to come with me."

Kate felt a slightly guilty sense of relief at being let off like this. "What shall I do instead?" she asked.

"Have a look around," Anne replied. "Explore the land. You might as well take advantage of the fine weather."

"Where can I go?" Kate asked.

"Anywhere."

"But it can't all be Grandma's land."

"Of course not. The farm is only thirty acres."

"How much is that?"

"I don't know what it is in modern measurements – we never learnt them at school – but it's enough to spend the whole day walking around."

Kate looked at her in astonishment. "Were your parents rich then?" she asked.

Anne laughed. "They certainly were not. Thirty acres is a very small farm. You need a lot of land for farming."

Kate thought about this. She supposed it must be true, if Anne said so. It still seemed incredible to her, that she could spend the whole day walking around the land and yet it was only a small farm. She thought about the tiny little gardens people had in London. It seemed an extraordinary contrast.

"What if I go on to someone else's land?" she asked.

"They won't mind."

"Are you sure?"

"Sure and certain," Anne said. "They don't worry about that sort of thing around here. Just shut any gates after you, that's all."

After breakfast Kate put on her coat and went outside. In front of the house the land sloped downwards and behind it, it rose steeply. As far as she could see there were fields, but the view ahead of her was interrupted by a line of trees.

Anne came out and stood behind her. "Which way should I go?" Kate asked.

"Why don't you go up to the turf bog?" Anne suggested.

"What's the turf bog?"

"It's where we used to cut the turf when I was a child. You know, the stuff that we burn in the stove?"

"Oh yes."

"There's a path behind the house that goes up to it."

"What's it like?"

"It's just hillside, wild and a bit wet in places but

51

you'll be all right if you stick to the path."

"Is it nice?"

"I used to think so, when I was a little girl. I used to go with my father to help him build the turf."

"What does that mean – build it?"

"He'd cut it out with a special spade and then I'd stand it in little groups of three so that the wind would dry it. When it was dry we used to bring it down with a donkey and cart."

"Did you have a donkey?" Kate asked with a rush of jealousy.

"Only when I was very little. My father got a tractor later on."

"Is the tractor still here?"

Anne shook her head. "That was how he was killed," she said. "The tractor overturned."

They stood together in silence. Kate was uncertain what she should say. She was not used to hearing about Anne's life.

"You could pick bilberries," Anne said, breaking the silence at last.

"What are bilberries?"

"Have you never seen them? I suppose you wouldn't have. They're little berries. They're all over the hillside. It might be a bit early for them yet."

"What do they look like?"

"I'll show you." Anne led the way down the drive and out on to the road. She turned left and began walking up the hill. There were no pavements to walk on, only a narrow grass verge and then hedgerows. After a short while there was a gap in the hedge. "This is the path up to the turf bog," Anne said.

Kate looked up the path. It was just about wide enough for a single car to pass but no car could come up here. The surface of the path was mud and stones and the grass was growing up through it. On either side were ditches down which water was trickling. Beyond the ditches there were more hedges and trees, screening the path from the fields on either side. In some places the trees grew right over the path and formed a canopy, leaving a green twilight underneath.

"This was all different when I lived here," Anne said. She sounded sad. "It's all got overgrown."

"I like it like this," Kate said.

"Pretty soon there will be no path at all," Anne said. "Anyway, there's nothing we can do about it. Let's go and see if we can find any bilberries." She walked up the path and began peering at the banks on either side. Then she stopped. "Here's one," she said. Kate bent down beside her. Anne showed her the very undistinguished plant growing beside the rock.

"But where are the berries?" Kate demanded.

"Under the leaves generally," Anne said. "Look." She produced a small purple berry about the size of a blackcurrant and handed it to Kate who popped it in her mouth.

"It's nice," Kate said. The taste was sharp, fruity but somehow earthy as well. "Are there any more?"

"Not on this plant," Anne said, standing up, "but up near the turf bog you should find loads of them. Carry on up this path until you come to a gate. There's a gap in the hedge on your left. If you go through that and across the field, you'll find the turf bog." She put her hand in her pocket and drew out a key. She handed it to Kate. "This is the front door key," she said. "Now don't lose it. I'll only be an hour or two." She leaned forward, kissed Kate on the cheek, turned and walked back down the path towards the road.

Kate carried on up the path, trying to imagine what it had been like when Anne was little. The grass grew tallest in the middle of the track. It wasn't really grass at all, but something like rushes. On either side, where the wheels of the cart and later the tractor had driven, very little grew. But in the middle it stood up in clumps of tall green spears. Kate broke one off, held it between her finger and thumb and threw it like a dart. She pictured Anne and her father driving a donkey and cart up the hill and coming back again in the evening with a load of turf.

In the distance she heard the sound of a car engine being started up. That must be Anne leaving. She paused and listened as the sound of the car grew more and more distant until she could no longer hear it. It was perfectly still except for the sound of water trickling down the ditch. She carried on up the path, pausing every now and again to search for bilberries.

It was harder work than she had expected, just walking upwards. She began to break out into a sweat and flies were buzzing around her face. She stopped for a rest, and as she did so she noticed a particularly good patch of bilberries growing on a bank on the other side of the ditch. Kate leaned forwards to reach them, but found she couldn't quite manage. She knew that if she leaned any further forwards she would fall into the ditch. It was only a few inches deep, but she didn't want to get wet. She gave up. A little further up, she came across a spot where the ditch was narrower and there was a gap in the hedge, through which she could see into the neighbouring field. She decided to try to cross the ditch, push her way through the hedge and go back along the other side of the hedge to see if she could reach the bilberries that way.

Kate put out her foot and stepped on to the bank on the other side of the ditch. But getting one foot across proved an awful lot easier than getting both feet across. She stood there, with one foot on either side of the ditch, uncertain what to do next. The bank on the far side was too steep to allow her to balance properly. She couldn't remain like this for ever, however. So, taking a deep breath, she brought her other foot across. Immediately she lost her footing altogether and slid downwards, both feet landing in the icy water. She squealed as the cold water soaked in through her trainers. Frantically she scrabbled up the bank again and pushed her way through the hedge. Brambles tore at her and a branch whipped her in the face, just below the eye.

At last she was through into the field, but even then her troubles weren't over. The land, she discovered, was far from dry. As she took a step forward she felt herself sinking in mud. She let out a cry and sprang backwards, but everywhere seemed to be the same. She plunged about, her feet sinking in wherever she trod. Cattle must have been walking here, she realised, for the marks of their hooves were everywhere, and as she stumbled backwards she found herself treading in cow dung. The disgusting smell of it broke over her, making her want to be sick.

At last she managed to find her way on to firmer ground. There was no question now of looking for bilberries. She would have to go back to the house and get cleaned up. The trouble was she couldn't get back on to the path again for that would mean going back through the boggy ground. She would have to make her way back through the fields. It couldn't be that difficult. As long as she kept in a straight line, she couldn't really go wrong.

With every step that she took, her feet squelched in her shoes and all the time she was aware of the horrible smell of cow dung. She began to feel cold too. Out here in the open ground there was no shelter from the wind, which was surprisingly strong.

She soon saw, too, that her plan to keep in a straight line was not going to work out. She came up against a barbed-wire fence running at right angles to the path. She stood confronting it, wondering if she could perhaps climb over it, but it was too high. Finally she decided that the only way was underneath. She took hold of the bottom strand of wire and pulled it upwards. It made some room, but not much. The problem was that she could not hold the wire up for herself and wriggle underneath it. She let go of the wire and lay down on the damp ground. She lifted the wire as much as she could with her right arm and shuffled forwards. She managed to get her head and one shoulder underneath, but she had to let go of the wire to get her other shoulder through. When she did, the wire caught on the back of her jacket. She was stuck.

She wanted to cry then, but she knew it wouldn't help. She was in the middle of the field. There was no one within earshot. It was up to her to get herself out. She had to stay calm and deal with it. She was lying on her front now and she tried to reach behind and unsnag the wire, but she put her hand on one of the barbs and cried out with pain. She stopped again and tried to think what would be the best thing she could do. Then she had an idea. It was her jacket that was attached to the wire. Perhaps she could wriggle out of it and escape that way. Once she was on the other side she could get her coat off separately. But it wasn't as easy as it had seemed at first. Her jacket had a zip up the front and she had to push her chest and stomach up off the ground and raise herself on to her elbows, or at least onto her forearms. She couldn't raise herself very much because the wire was pressed against her back. She took a deep breath, pushed herself up, fumbled with the zip and got it partly undone, before she had to lie down flat again to get her breath. Then she took another breath and tried again. Somehow she managed to unzip the jacket and wriggle her arms out of the sleeves. At last she was free. She pushed herself forwards until she was clear of the wire. Then she struggled to her feet. She was covered in mud and scratched, but she had got through the fence. She bent down again, unhooked her jacket and put it on.

That was when she saw the boy. He was some distance away, but he must have been watching her. As she stood there, he came nearer and she saw that he was about her own age, or a little older. He had brown, curly hair and he was wearing jeans, a thick jumper and a jacket. "Hello," he said.

Kate felt herself blushing scarlet. "Hello," she said. She knew that she must have looked absolutely ridiculous, wriggling under the fence with her bottom in the air, covered in mud with a torn coat, bits of grass stuck in her hair and scratches all over her. Then she remembered, too, that she stank of cow dung. She began backing away as the boy approached. He stopped. "There's a gate just up there," he said, pointing with his thumb.

As the meaning of his words sank into her Kate felt the most complete fool.

"You must be Mrs Gallagher's daughter," he continued. It was funny to hear Anne called Mrs Gallagher.

She nodded, still backing away from him. "I've got to go back to the house," she said.

"It's that way," the boy said, pointing back the way he had come. "I could come with you, if you like."

He was trying to be nice, she could see that, but she had to get away. She didn't want to talk to anyone. She just wanted to get home and get clean.

"No, thank you," she said, edging around him in a big circle. She began to walk rapidly away.

"The name's Liam," the boy called after her.

"Goodbye," she called back.

The field was sloping downwards, and as soon as he was out of sight over the hill, she began to run. The urge to get home was all-consuming. She strode along through the field, keeping the line of the path on her left. At last the house came in sight. She had come round to the back of it and there was a low stone wall between the back garden and the field. In the wall was an iron gate. She pushed open the gate and walked into the back garden.

She stood on the doorstep fumbling in her pocket for the key, and now that it was all over, for some reason she found hot tears running down her face. Sobbing out loud, she opened the door and flung herself inside.

Chapter Six

KATE HAD just finished drying herself when Anne came home an hour later, but at least she was clean. She still felt scratched, sore and smarting with embarrassment but she had scrubbed herself from head to toe until her skin was pink.

"Anyone at home?" Anne called out.

"I'm upstairs."

Kate pulled on a T-shirt and a skirt, then quickly squirted herself with some of Anne's perfume. She went downstairs.

"You smell nice," Anne said. She was filling up the kettle under the tap.

"Thank you."

"In fact, isn't that my perfume?"

"Yes." Anne didn't like Kate using her perfume. "You can have your own perfume," she had protested when Kate had put it on to go to a party, "but mine is for me. I'm older than you and I need a different kind of perfume."

Kate felt this was not entirely fair, but she did what Anne wanted and bought her own perfume, cheaper than Anne's, out of her pocket money. Unfortunately she had left it in England. It hadn't occurred to her that she would really want to use it on the first day there.

"Sorry," Kate said. She explained about the cow dung.

"That's the trouble with cows," Anne said with a smile. "They have no manners."

Kate wasn't amused. "It was disgusting," she said. "My jeans are ruined."

"Did you only bring one pair?" Anne asked.

"Yes."

"That wasn't very clever."

"Well how was I to know the place was going to be covered in cow dung?" Kate demanded angrily.

"It's not covered in cow dung," Anne said. "Don't exaggerate."

"And then, when I got home," Kate continued, "there was a huge spider in the bath."

"My God!" Anne said, in mock horror. "How did you survive?"

"That isn't funny," Kate said. "And the water was brown."

"The water here *is* brown," Anne told her. "It's perfectly all right."

"How can it be perfectly all right if it's brown?"

"It's minerals that make it brown. That's all. Around here they call it iron water."

Kate did not feel convinced. "How long will we have to stay here?" she asked.

Anne shrugged. She set about making a cup of tea. "I don't know," she said. "She was awake this morning."

"Your mother?"

"Yes."

Kate hoped that meant they could go home soon. "Is she better?" she asked.

"No. She's very far from being better."

"But she will get better?"

"I don't know. Possibly. Possibly not."

"But she's awake?" Kate insisted.

"Yes," Anne admitted, "but she can't talk. Her tongue is paralysed."

This was a horrible thing to think about.

"She can't eat," Anne went on. "She will still have to be fed by a tube. And there may be other paralysis as well."

"What do you mean?"

"Other parts of her body might be paralysed. They don't know yet because she's too weak to move."

Kate was not sure what she should feel. It was hard to feel sad about this news. She had never had any contact with her grandmother before and even now she was just an old woman lying in a bed. She wondered how Anne felt about it.

"The next twenty-four hours is critical. Some people do recover, some don't. We'll just have to wait and see," Anne said, pouring boiling water into the teapot.

"There was a boy in the field," Kate said.

"One of Aidan's I suppose," Anne said. "Did he tell you his name?"

"Liam."

"I think he's the youngest," Anne said.

"What was he doing in Grandma's fields?" Kate asked.

"I don't know. Looking for sheep, perhaps. They keep sheep. Or he might have been looking for something else." She smiled and looked knowingly at Kate.

"Such as what?" Kate said, determined not to go along with Anne's joke.

"Such as any young English girls he might come across," her mother suggested.

"Don't be silly," Kate said.

"I'm not," Anne insisted. "News travels fast in a small community. Do you want some tea?"

"No thanks. Well, I don't suppose he was very impressed with what he found," she said.

"I shouldn't give up all hope," Anne replied. She seemed determined to carry on teasing, whatever Kate said.

"I'm not hoping for anything," Kate said. She sat

down crossly on a chair opposite her mother. "I just want to go home," she said.

"I know how you feel," Anne told her.

"No you don't," Kate insisted. "How could you?" Even as she spoke she knew that she was being unfair, but she couldn't help herself.

"Listen," Anne said. "Why don't we have some lunch and then go into town. We could get you some wellingtons."

"I don't want any wellingtons," Kate said.

"You'll need them if you're going to go walking around the fields," Anne told her.

"I'm not going to go walking around the fields again."

"We could look for some new jeans," Anne suggested.

"They won't have any."

"Of course they will," Anne said. "Don't be so stuck-up."

"I wasn't being stuck-up," Kate said indignantly. If there was one thing she could say about herself it was that she wasn't stuck-up. Her friend Laura was inclined to be a bit stuck-up. She sometimes looked at the clothes Kate bought as if they were cheap. She always bought expensive clothes. But Kate didn't care. She liked nice things but she didn't look down on people just because they couldn't afford them. That was what being stuck-up meant and she was not stuck-up.

"Just because it's a little town in the west of Ireland, doesn't mean they haven't heard of jeans," Anne said.

"I didn't say they hadn't heard of them. I just meant that they might not have the ones I like," Kate finished lamely.

"Well why don't we see?" Anne said with the air of someone who has just won the argument.

"If you like," Kate replied. There was no point in arguing with Anne.

Chapter Seven

THEY PASSED very few cars on the way to Cruachan. To Kate's surprise the drivers of those that they did pass, raised a hand in greeting. The third time this happened she asked Anne about it. "Do you know those people?" she said.

"No."

"But they waved to you."

"People do that around here," Anne said. "Everybody knows everybody else. I expect they're waving to the car. They know it's Nora Gallagher's and they assume I must be her daughter."

"Does everybody around here know absolutely everybody else?"

"More or less," Anne said. "Until we get to the Four Mile Cross, anyway."

"What's the Four Mile Cross?"

"It's a cross roads four miles outside of Cruachan. Between here and there most of the families have been living in the same place for generations."

"Wow!" Kate said. It seemed such a strange idea.

Cruachan town looked to Kate like an overgrown village. It was not even as busy or as sophisticated as the shopping centre in the part of London where she and Anne lived.

"This is where I used to come every weekend when I was your age," Anne said.

"Here?"

"This was the centre of my little world."

They parked by a grocery shop and went inside. The shop seemed to sell everything and anything. Tools were side by side with biscuits. There were plastic bottles that looked like feeding bottles for babies but had a picture of a man feeding a sheep on the wrapping. There were parts for tractors alongside cans of soups, exercise books and newspapers. "This is a weird shop," Kate said to herself.

The man who owned the shop came out in a white overall. "Hello there," he said. He looked at Anne for a moment then he said, "Aren't you Nora Gallagher's daughter?"

"I am," Anne told him.

"You're welcome home," he said.

"Thank you," Anne replied.

"I remember you when you were only going to school," the man went on.

Anne laughed at him. "Is that right?" she said.

"It is," he said. His face, which had been smiling,

grew grave. "I was awful sorry to hear about your mother," he said.

"Thank you," Anne replied.

"How's she making out?"

"We don't know yet," Anne told him. "The next day or two will tell."

"We're all keeping our fingers crossed," he assured her.

Anne had made a list of things that she wanted and, as she read them out he fetched them and put them into a carrier-bag for her. When she had finished, Kate went over to join her. She saw a sign advertising stamps. "Can I have seven first-class stamps, please?" she asked.

"You can of course," the man said. He took them out of a box beneath the counter. "And is this your little girl?" he asked Anne.

Kate scowled at him. Another one who seemed to think she was about six.

"It is," Anne said.

"She's like yourself, anyway," the man said, taking the money Anne offered him and sorting out the change.

"Do you think so?"

"The living image." He smiled at them both and handed the change to Anne and the stamps to Kate.

Outside the shop, Kate took the letters she had written out of her pocket and, one by one, she stuck stamps on them.

"That's an awful lot of letters," Anne remarked.

"I suppose it is," Kate said. "Where can I post them?"

"There's a post box just across the road," Anne said.

Kate looked in the direction she had indicated. "It's green!" she exclaimed in surprise. "It looks just like an English post box, but it's been painted green instead of red."

"It is an English post box," Anne said.

"But why?"

"The whole of Ireland used to be ruled by England once," Anne said. "Didn't they teach you that at school?"

"Sort of, I think," Kate said.

"Afterwards, when they got independence, it was one of the first things they did, change the colour of the letter boxes."

While Kate posted her letters, Anne put their bags in the boot of the car. Then she led the way to a shop which had the name McGrisken's Outfitters written above the window. In the window ancient-looking dummies were wearing outfits that looked as if they came from a time before the war.

"This place isn't any good," Kate said.

"It'll be all right inside," Kate told her.

It was dark inside the shop. A middle-aged woman was sitting behind a counter reading the newspaper.

Behind her, clothes were stacked in boxes and on shelves. She looked up as they came in.

"Can I help you?" she asked.

Anne explained that they were looking for a pair of jeans for Kate.

The woman looked Kate up and down with a knowledgeable eye. Then she turned round and took a pair of jeans off a shelf behind her. She unfolded them and handed them to Kate. "There's a changing room at the back," she said.

To Kate's surprise the jeans fitted perfectly and they were a good shape. When she came out of the changing room wearing them, Anne smiled and nodded. "They're great," she said.

Anne and Kate disagreed about a lot of things but one thing they shared was taste. If Kate liked the way something looked, she could be sure that Anne would too. Some of her friends had absolutely nothing in common with their parents, but Anne and Kate were quite close like that. Perhaps that was another reason why people often mistook them for sisters.

"We need some wellingtons too," Anne said.

"What size?" the woman asked.

Kate told her and the woman produced a pair of green wellingtons. "Is that everything?" she asked.

Kate had noticed a selection of jumpers, hanging from a rail. They were big and chunky, a bit like the one the boy in the field had been wearing. She liked them. "How much are these?" she asked.

The woman told her the price. Kate looked at Anne. "If you like," Anne said.

Kate tried on three of the jumpers before she found one that was perfect. It was a dark red colour. Red always suited Kate.

"What shall we do now?" Kate asked after they had paid for the clothes and left the shop. Although she had initially been reluctant to make the journey into Cruachan, she didn't want to go home again so soon.

"We could go and have a cup of coffee," Anne suggested.

"OK."

Kate expected Anne to lead the way to a café or a restaurant, but they headed instead for a bar. It was dark and smoky inside and full of people sitting at small round tables or standing at the bar. They were laughing and joking or just sitting, staring in front of them at glasses of beer. "Are you sure they serve coffee in here?" Kate asked.

"Of course they do," Anne told her. "You sit down there. I'll go and order."

Kate sat down at the empty table Anne had indicated and looked around her. The walls were panelled with dark wood. The ceiling was low and painted a pale brown colour. The place felt as if it was underground.

Anne came back carrying a tray with two cups of coffee, a jug of cream and a bowl of sugar lumps.

Absent-mindedly Kate took one of the sugar lumps and popped it into her mouth.

"You shouldn't do that," Anne protested.

"I know."

"It's bad for your teeth. And, besides, it's not very grown up."

"OK, OK," Kate said. "It was only a sugar lump."

"It's just a bad habit, that's all," Anne went on.

Kate sighed. Anne could be so nice, like in the shop just now when she had bought the jumper for Kate without batting an eyelid, but she could also be such a pain. She always knew best. That was her worst quality. "I have to have some fun, you know," Kate told her.

"Eating sugar isn't having fun," Anne said. "It's just being greedy."

Kate said nothing. She just gave Anne one of her looks. Somehow the afternoon, which had looked as if it was going to turn out all right, was going the same way as the morning.

"How are you doing, Anne?" a voice said.

A woman was standing next to their table, smiling down at them.

"Bridget!" Anne exclaimed.

"You haven't changed one bit," the woman went on.

"There must be something wrong with your eyes then," Anne said.

73

"There's nothing wrong with my eyes at all." She turned to Kate. "You must be Kathleen."

"Kate."

"I'm sorry. Kate. You're just like your mother, do you know that?"

Kate shook her head.

"The living image. Well you're very welcome to Cruachan anyhow." She held out her hand to Kate who shook it.

"Pull over a chair and sit down," Anne said.

"Only for a minute. I haven't really got time to stop. I was just on my way out when I caught sight of the pair of you sitting there. That's Anne Gallagher, I said to myself, and I had to come over and talk to you." She turned to Kate. "This woman and I sat next to each other in school," she said. "She was the one with the brains, mind you, and the looks as well."

"Get away with you," Anne said. Kate looked at her in surprise. More and more of her mother's English-ness seemed to be disappearing with each day she spent here.

"It's the truth," Bridget went on. "She had every boy in the place after her."

Kate thought about this. It did not fit in at all with the image of her mother that she knew, but then perhaps there was more than one Anne Gallagher.

Although she had said that she had no time to talk, Bridget showed no sign of leaving. She sat there rattling on about her and Anne's schooldays, breaking out every few seconds into great gusts of laughter. Suddenly she looked at her watch and jumped up as if she had been stung by a bee. "I've got to go," she said. "I've a houseful at home waiting for me." She turned to Kate. "You must be bored stiff in that house all day on your own."

"I'm OK," Kate said.

"I'll send Siobhan over to see you," Bridget said, ignoring her response. "She's my sister's daughter. I have her staying with me at the moment. She's the same age as yourself, more or less. She'll show you the sights. Well, I'll love you and leave you, Anne. It was great seeing you again. Pop over when you get a chance." And without waiting for a reply from either of them, she was gone.

On the way back home, Kate said, "I liked that woman."

"Bridget? She's lovely."

"She talks a lot, doesn't she?"

"Never stops. She was always in trouble at school."

They had passed the Four Mile Cross by now and the driver of the first car they saw raised his hand in greeting.

"I can't get over the way everybody here knows everybody else."

"It's like that in any small community," Anne told her.

"I suppose so. It must be hard to keep any secrets though."

"Why do you think I left?" Anne said.

Kate blushed. "I thought you left because Grandma made you," she said.

"She didn't make me."

"What happened then?"

Anne shrugged. "It was the easiest thing, I suppose," she said.

They drove on in silence. Kate felt uncomfortable. It was as if she was responsible for uprooting her mother from her family and friends. It made her feel guilty and angry at the same time. After all, she hadn't asked to be born.

"Are you sorry you left?" Kate asked when they had pulled up outside the house.

Anne turned and looked at her in surprise. "Sorry I left?" she repeated, as if the words didn't quite make sense. She sat there for a moment thinking about the question. Then she shook her head. "No," she said. "I'm not sorry I left, not at all. But I think perhaps I'm just beginning to be glad that I came back."

Chapter Eight

THE NEXT day Bridget was as good as her word. Just after breakfast there was a knock on the door and when Kate went to open it she found a girl about the same age as herself, a little taller with red hair and freckles. "Hi," she said. "I'm Siobhan."

They went inside and Kate introduced her to Anne.

"Hello, Siobhan," Anne said. "You're bright and early. We were just finishing breakfast. Have you had some?"

Siobhan said she had already had breakfast but she wouldn't mind a piece of toast. She seemed to have no difficulty at all in talking to people she had met for the first time. She sat down at the table with them and was soon spreading jam thickly on to her slice of toast. Kate wondered if *she* would have been able to introduce herself like this and just walk in. She felt sure that she would not.

"Do you live in London?" Siobhan asked.

"Yes."

"That must be wonderful."

"Why do you say that?" Kate asked.

"Well, you know, London, the big city."

"It's OK," Kate said.

"Have you met anyone around here yet?" Siobhan went on, munching her toast at the same time.

"This is only my second day," Kate informed her.

"That's long enough around here," Siobhan said.

"I met a boy in the fields yesterday. He said his name was Liam."

"He's nice," Siobhan said.

"Well I think I'd better be getting off to the hospital," Anne said, finishing her tea and standing up. She began picking up the plates from the table.

"Don't worry about that," Siobhan said. "We'll clear up, won't we?" She looked at Kate.

"Yes," Kate said, a little uncertainly. She wasn't at all sure how to react to Siobhan. They had only met her five minutes ago and already she was taking charge of the house.

But Anne didn't seem worried. "Good," she said. She picked up her coat from where it was draped over the banisters. "I'll leave you two to get on with it then. I'll be back in a couple of hours."

After Anne had gone and Kate and Siobhan had finished clearing up, Siobhan said, "Do you fancy going to a sheep-shearing?"

"A sheep-shearing?" Kate repeated doubtfully.

"It's a laugh. Liam will be there."

"Where is it being held?"

"At the Dooleys'. It's the next farm along."

Kate shrugged. "OK," she said.

Together they left the house and set off down the drive. They turned up the hill and walked along the road, past the path that led up to the turf bog.

"Is this your first time in Ireland?" Siobhan asked.

"Yes."

"My aunt said it was."

Kate wondered what else Siobhan's aunt might have said about her.

"She used to sit next to your mum at school," Siobhan went on. "They were great friends, did you know?"

"Yes," Kate said.

"My aunt says that your mum was really popular in our village."

Kate suddenly began to feel angry. She had a feeling that Siobhan meant something else when she said 'popular'.

"What do you mean?" she demanded.

Siobhan looked at her in surprise. "I mean everybody liked her. They were really sad when she went away."

Kate looked at Siobhan's face as she spoke and realised that she meant what she was saying, that and only that. "I thought you meant ..." Kate began. She wasn't sure how to carry on.

Siobhan looked puzzled.

"Oh, nothing," she said. The conversation seemed to have fallen into a big hole and the two girls walked along in silence.

"Oh, look at the Christmas trees!" Kate said, trying to change the subject. On either side of the road Christmas trees were growing. She looked more closely. "They're growing in rows," she said. It was true, the trees by the side of the road were growing in straight lines.

"It's a tree farm," Siobhan said.

"A what?"

"A tree farm. They grow the trees like any other crop," Siobhan said. "I think they're very ugly."

"But I thought trees took ever such a long time to grow," Kate said.

"They do."

"Then how can it be like a farm?"

"It's a fifteen-year cycle," Siobhan said. "And you should see the mess the land is left in afterwards. It's no good for anything."

"You really don't like them," Kate said, surprised.

"Of course not," Siobhan told her. "Nobody likes them around here."

"But I thought woods were good," Kate said. "You know, for the environment. And they look pretty."

"If you like fields full of Christmas trees," Siobhan

said, "I suppose they're all right. Nobody round here likes them, though. My dad says they'd plant the whole of Cruachan, if they could."

"Would they?" Kate asked in astonishment.

"Some people would, if they could get enough money out of it," Siobhan said.

"What sort of people?" Kate asked.

"The likes of Dennis Carthy," Siobhan told her.

"Who's Dennis Carthy?" Kate asked.

"The fellow who owns this tree farm," Siobhan said. Then she added, "What did you think of Liam?"

"Who?"

"The boy you met in the fields."

"Oh him. I didn't think anything of him."

"I like him," Siobhan said. "And his friend Sean. He's really nice."

Kate smiled. She decided that she liked Siobhan. She was so open. "Do you live in Cruachan?" she asked.

"I live on the other side of the town from here," Siobhan said. "But I come to stay with my aunt a lot. There's more going on around here."

"What sort of things?" Kate asked. She couldn't imagine very much going on. There were hardly any houses.

"Oh, you know, people meet up, have a laugh."

They carried on walking for what seemed like a long time. At last Siobhan announced that they had arrived. They drew level with another path which branched off the road to their left. Just inside the opening was a big, five-bar gate. Siobhan pulled back the bolt and it swung open with a creak.

They followed the path and came out into a farm-yard. The first thing that Kate noticed was sheep. They were everywhere, milling around bleating, getting in each other's way. Two big sheep dogs were running around them, barking. It looked like complete chaos to Kate.

Someone called to the dogs and immediately they retreated to a corner of the yard and sat there with their tongues hanging out and big grins on their faces. Kate realised, with a start, who it was that the dogs belonged to. It was the boy she had met in the field. She quickly looked away but she knew that he had recognised her.

"There's Liam," Siobhan said.

"Are those his dogs?"

"Not really. They're his brother Michael's. He's the sheep shearer. Shall we go inside and watch?"

"OK," Kate agreed. She followed Siobhan across the courtyard, pushing her way through the frightened animals. As she did so, she couldn't resist putting her hand out to touch one. It immediately darted to one side, but not before she had found that it felt exactly as she would have expected: woolly and springy.

As she drew near the barn, Kate could hear a low humming noise which grew louder as they drew nearer.

It stopped when they went inside.

Inside the barn there were still more sheep penned in behind a sort of gate or hurdle. One by one they were being sheared. A young man was standing holding a sheep with one hand. In the other he held a pair of electric shears. He looked up when the two girls came in.

"Hello, yourselves," he said.

"Hello, Michael," Siobhan said. "This is Kate."

"How's it going, Kate?" Michael said.

"Great," she said. She wasn't sure if that was the right thing to say, but Michael didn't seem to need an answer. He immediately turned his attention back to the sheep in front of him. He turned the clippers on and the buzzing noise they had heard outside filled the barn.

It was funny watching the wool coming off the sheep. Michael didn't cut it off in bits, the way a hairdresser cuts a person's hair. Instead he deftly worked the clippers round the sheep so that all of a sudden the fleece came away in one go. As he let go of the sheep he looked up at her and saw her fascination. He turned off the shears, "Would you like to have a go?" he asked.

"Me?"

"Who else?" He grinned, and she knew that he was not making fun of her but trying to be friendly.

"OK," she said.

The sheep, looking very much trimmer, was let out

of the barn and Michael selected another one from behind the pen. He shooed it over to the shearing area. Kate looked at the sheep uncertainly. Was she supposed to capture it? she wondered.

"Don't worry, I'll hold it for you," Michael told her. He bent down and seized the sheep expertly, pinning it with an arm and a leg. "They're not frightened if you're not," he said.

Kate was pleased to hear this. She had been worried that the poor silly creature would be terrified.

Michael picked up the shears and turned them on. Again the buzzing filled the barn.

"Like this, see." He showed her how to work the clippers.

"What if I ruin it?" Kate said.

"You won't," Michael assured her.

"But if I do?"

"What the hell? There's plenty more of them."

She placed the shears against the side of the sheep, where he showed her, and held them as the blades cut into the wool. They wanted to run away with her, like a lawnmower, but she kept them under control. Very gently, Michael put his hand over hers and guided it as she cut carefully through the fleece. She knew that it was him, not her, who was doing the shearing, but at the same time she felt a sense of satisfaction as the fleece began to lift off like a carpet until finally there was hardly any of it still attached to the sheep and then, with a final cut, the fleece came away in one.

Michael turned off the trimmers. "There now," he told her. "That wasn't bad at all, for a beginner."

"You did it," she told him, but she was pleased at what he had said. She stayed, watching as all the sheep in the barn were sheared, one after the other. Then Michael turned off the shears, leaned his head out of the door and shouted to his brother to send in more sheep.

"Let's go and talk to Liam," Siobhan said.

She led the way across the yard, to where Liam was standing. He was whistling to the dogs and they seemed to understand the whistles. One of them kept most of the sheep at one end of the yard while the other dog rounded up a small group of them and herded them through the door of the barn. After the operation was complete and Michael had shut the door of the barn, Liam whistled to the dogs again. They lay down on the ground.

"Those dogs of yours are nearly human, Liam," Siobhan said, as she walked over to join him.

Kate followed behind. She still felt embarrassed because of their meeting in the field, when she had been filthy, smelling of cow dung and not far from tears.

Liam looked pleased with this compliment. "They're good dogs, all right," he said.

"This is Kate," Siobhan told him.

"How's it going?" Liam said.

"OK," Kate said.

"This is her first time in Ireland," Siobhan went on.

"And how do you like it?" Liam asked her.

"It's lovely," Kate said. She surprised herself by the answer. Up until very recently she had been thinking how much she disliked it here.

"You're from London, aren't you?" Liam asked.

"Yes."

"That must be great."

"Why does everybody say that?" Kate asked.

Liam shrugged. "Well, you know, London ..." he said, as if it needed no explaining.

"Her mother and my aunt went to school together," Siobhan said.

"I know that," Liam told her. "And my dad, too. But he was older."

"Does everybody really know everybody else around here?" Kate asked them.

"Pretty much," Liam agreed. "Is it true your mother runs a big restaurant?"

"No," Kate said. "She runs a little café."

"That sounds brilliant."

"It's OK," Kate said. "It's hard work, actually."

"As hard as farming?" Liam asked with a half-smile, as if he thought this was very unlikely.

"Harder than whistling at dogs anyway," Kate said, just a little bit annoyed with him.

Liam did not look at all put out by her answer.

"One up to you," he said. "How long are you staying?"

"I don't know. Until my grandmother gets better, I suppose."

Liam seemed pleased at this. "You'll be here a good while yet then," he said.

"I suppose I will," Kate said.

That was the moment when Kate suddenly realised that she felt happy. It was a feeling that she hadn't known for days, ever since that first phone call to Emma, when she had learned that her friends had gone swimming and left her out. She realised that Liam, Michael and Siobhan wanted her to be here. They liked her, even though they knew almost nothing about her. "It's because I'm new," she thought to herself.

"Liam, have the puppies been born yet?" Siobhan asked.

"That's old news," Liam said. "Do you want to see them?" He looked at Kate as well as Siobhan when he spoke.

"We do, of course," Siobhan told him, and Kate nodded in agreement.

The puppies were in another barn, lying on straw against their mother. "They're beautiful," Kate exclaimed. "How many are there?"

"Six," Liam said ruefully. "And we have to find homes for all of them."

"Aren't you going to keep any of them?"

"Three dogs is enough for one farm," Liam said.

"But will you be able to find homes for all of them?" Kate asked.

Liam nodded. "I'd say so," he said. "Our dogs are well thought of."

"Oh look!" Kate said suddenly as one of the puppies, which had been happily sucking at its mother's teat, was somehow shouldered away by its brothers and sisters and flopped around frantically trying to get back. Liam bent down and put it back.

"They'll all have to be trained," he said. "Up to a point, anyway. It'll be madness around here when they get a bit bigger." Kate imagined the six puppies all grown up rushing around out in the yard, barking at each other. The thought made her smile.

Kate and Siobhan stayed on at the shearing for a long time. Liam said his friend Sean should be arriving at any moment, and it was obvious to Kate that Siobhan was keen to see him, but Sean didn't turn up and in the end hunger got the better of them and they set off home for lunch.

All the way back to her grandmother's house, Kate kept thinking about Liam. He wasn't the sort of boy she normally liked. He wasn't particularly tall, he wasn't dark, he didn't have sparkling blue eyes. If you had asked her what sort of a boy she fancied before she had left London, these were all characteristics she would have mentioned. Liam had none of these. He was just a little taller than herself. He had brown curly hair and his eyes were green. But there was something about him that seemed to grow on her. She felt a kind of rosy glow inside. Partly it was because everyone had been so nice to her, but there was more to it than that. She felt certain that Liam was particularly interested in her, even though he didn't say very much, and she liked the feeling.

When they reached the bottom of the lane that led to her grandmother's house, Siobhan explained that she had promised to help her aunt that afternoon.

"See you then," Kate said.

"What are you doing tomorrow?" Siobhan asked.

"I don't know," Kate replied. "I thought I might go in to the hospital with my mum in the morning." She didn't know exactly why she said this. Partly it was because she didn't know what else to say. She had no other life here in Ireland. In London she might have said that she was going to go shopping or swimming or that she was going round to one of her friend's houses. Over here she was just herself. Also she just sort of felt that it was the right thing to do. Even though her grandmother hadn't wanted to have anything to do with her, Kate wouldn't behave in the same way.

"Shall I come round in the afternoon?" Siobhan asked.

"Yes," Kate said. "That would be good."

"See you tomorrow, then."

"See you."

Siobhan went off down the road.

Kate was looking forward to telling Anne about the sheep-shearing and the puppies, but her thoughts stopped abruptly when she opened the front door and heard a man's voice. She immediately assumed it must be Aidan, Liam's and Michael's father who had met them at the station, but when she went into the front room she saw that Anne was talking to a stranger. Unlike Aidan, who dressed like she imagined a farmer would dress, in old weather-stained clothes, this man was wearing a suit. He stood up when she came into the room. That surprised her. She wasn't accustomed to adults standing up when she went into a room.

"This is my daughter, Kate," Anne said. "Kate, this is Dennis Carthy."

The name was immediately familiar, even though Kate was perfectly sure she had never set eyes on this man before. She tried to think where she had heard of him.

Dennis Carthy held out his hand very formally. Kate took it and he squeezed her hand in a very firm handshake. Too firm, in fact. It felt uncomfortable. Kate withdrew her hand. "Hello," she said.

"And how do you like Ireland?" Dennis Carthy asked her.

Kate was beginning to get tired of being asked this. "It's different," she said.

He nodded. "It would be of course." Then he turned to Anne. "I won't keep you any longer," he said. "You will think about what I said though, won't you?"

"I'll think about it," Anne said.

"Good. Nice to have met you." He went out of the door and Anne followed, to close it behind him.

Then Kate remembered where she had heard the name. He was the man who owned the tree farm.

"What did he want?" Kate asked her mother when she came back.

"He wanted me to sell him the land," Anne said.

"Sell him the land?" Kate repeated. "But could you? I mean, it's not yours to sell, is it?"

"No," Anne said. "That was what I told him. Shall we have lunch? I'm starving."

One thing that Anne could do was cook. She could whip up something absolutely marvellous out of next to nothing. Soon they were sitting down to one of Kate's favourites: eggs mexicane.

"This is lovely," Kate said. "All that walking really gives you an appetite." She had told Anne all about the sheep and about the puppies as they prepared the meal together. Suddenly she thought of the tree farm again and of Dennis Carthy. "What did he mean, just before he left?" she asked Anne.

"Who?"

"Dennis Carthy. He said, 'You will think about what I said, won't you?'."

"Oh that." Anne sighed. "He wants me to think about getting power of attorney."

"Getting what?"

"Power of attorney. It's a legal term," Anne explained. "It means that I am empowered to act on my mother's behalf. It's what people do when someone becomes incapable of acting for themselves."

Kate thought about this. For some reason she did not like the idea at all. "But supposing Grandma recovers?" she asked.

"The process can be reversed," Anne told her.

"But what about the farm? If that's been sold, you won't be able to get it back."

"I know," Anne said. "I didn't agree to it. I just promised to think about it, that's all."

"I didn't like him," Kate said.

"You don't know anything about him."

"He's not popular with the local people," Kate pointed out.

Anne looked at her in surprise. "How do you know that?" she asked.

"Siobhan told me."

"Did she now? Well I certainly don't intend to do anything in a hurry. All right?"

Kate nodded.

"But we can't stay here for ever," Anne went on.

"Of course not."

"Goodness knows what might happen to the café."

"Nothing will happen to it," Kate assured her. "Marian can look after it perfectly well on her own."

"For a little while," Anne insisted. "Anyway, you were the one who couldn't wait to get back to London. You've changed your tune a bit, haven't you?"

"No. I just didn't like that man, that's all. He squeezed my hand too hard."

Anne laughed out loud. "Honestly, Kate," she said. "You do say the silliest things."

That night in her bedroom, Kate delved into her travelling bag and took out the chain letter. She read it over again, stopped at the bit that said "after some days a boy will ask you out or tell you he loves you". There was quite a difference between these two possibilities, but neither of them seemed terribly likely. The truth was that no boy had ever asked her out, not so far. Some of her friends had boyfriends and most of them had gone out with boys a few times, but not Kate, not yet. She didn't mind particularly. The boys at her school were all really awful anyway.

There was one time when she had thought that Darren Wates was going to ask her out. He was in the same year as her and he had sticking-out ears. One break time a group of boys stood around looking at her with Darren in the middle of them. They were giggling and making jokes that she couldn't hear properly. Somebody said, "Go on then," and Darren was shoved in her direction, but he just turned round and ran back towards his mates, lashing out at them as they splintered in all directions, laughing their heads off. Kate had just walked away without taking any notice of them. She wouldn't have gone out with him, anyway. He acted like he was about six years old all the time.

She folded the letter up and put it back in her travelling bag. At least she hadn't broken the chain. She had copied out the letter seven times like it told her to and posted the seven copies off. It couldn't do any harm. "And you never know," she said to herself. "Something might happen." She switched off the reading lamp and was asleep within minutes.

Chapter Nine

THE NEXT morning, as they were driving to the hospital, Kate asked, "What was my father like?" It was not the first time she had asked the question, but it was the first time for a long while. The reason for this was simple: she had found out as much as Anne seemed prepared to tell her.

"I've told you about him," Anne said. She didn't look at Kate as she spoke, but the tone of her voice was enough to tell Kate it was an unwelcome subject. Nevertheless Kate persisted.

"All I know was that his name was Joseph Hendry and that he was a musician."

Anne shrugged. "There isn't much else to tell you."

"There must be heaps more to tell," Kate said, exasperated.

"Why must there be?"

"Because there must. Did you love him?"

"I thought I did. For a little while."

"And did he love you?"

"He said he did, but he didn't know what the word meant. He was full of blarney."

"What does that mean – blarney?"

"Moonshine," Anne said. "Lovely sweet romantic nonsense."

"How do you know it was nonsense?"

"It's always nonsense," Anne said. "The world isn't like that."

"Sometimes it can be," Kate said. She didn't know exactly why she said that but she felt that it was true.

"You can't live on blarney," Anne told her. "You can't pay bills with it."

That was typical of Anne, Kate thought, reducing everything, even love, to common-sense matters like paying bills. She felt angry with Anne, as she always did on those occasions when she tried to broach this subject. At the same time she felt completely powerless. Trying to get Anne to do something or tell you something if she didn't want to was like beating your head against a brick wall. She wanted to ask "Didn't my father want me then?" but she couldn't bring herself to say the words. At the very thought of the question, tears began welling up inside her, filling the space behind her eyes. She swallowed hard and collected herself. Instead she asked a different question, one that was somehow easier to think about. "Was Grandma very angry when she found out that you were . . . you know?"

"Pregnant?" Anne completed the sentence for her.
"Yes."

"Not so much angry as shocked," Anne told her. "She couldn't accept that her little girl could really have grown up."

Kate thought about this. She couldn't help wondering how Anne would react if she, Kate, had found herself in the same position. Nothing more was said after that. They drove to the hospital in silence.

This time they knew their way to the room her grandmother was in. Kate was surprised, when they got there, to find that most of the tubes and apparatus had been removed. Her eyes were open, though they didn't seem focused on anything in particular. The nurse, who had been bending over the bed when they came into the room, straightened up and smiled at them. "She's been making really good progress," she told them. "Haven't you?" she said, turning to Kate's grandma. "See?" she said, turning back to Anne and Kate. "She understands every word I'm saying to her."

Kate was not sure how the nurse had come to that conclusion. She could see no flicker of recognition in the old woman's face when the nurse spoke to her.

"Talk to her," the nurse instructed them. "The more you talk to her, the quicker she's going to get better." She turned back to Kate's grandma. "I'll leave you with your visitors now," she said. She acted as if the woman on the bed was able to hear and speak just

97

like anyone else, which seemed strange to Kate, for it was obvious that though her grandmother was a great deal better, she was still a long, long way from being normal. Still, she supposed that was what you had to do: treat people as if they are well and hope that they will get well. She wondered if she would have the patience to be a nurse. She doubted it.

Anne sat down on one side of the bed and Kate sat down on the other. "Hello, Mum," Anne said. "I'm back and Kate's here too. Do you remember, I told you I'd brought her with me? Say hello, Kate."

"Hello," Kate said, looking at her grandmother. It was strange, talking to someone who didn't respond in any way.

They sat there in silence after that. In the background they could hear the everyday sounds of the hospital: the hum of machinery, the noise of someone wheeling a trolley in the corridor, the low murmur of voices discussing matters of life and death.

"Tell her about your trip up to the turf bog," Anne said.

"I didn't get as far as the turf bog."

"It doesn't matter."

So Kate began telling her grandmother about setting off to pick the bilberries and when she got to the bit where she had stepped in the cow dung, she found herself smiling. It no longer seemed such a dreadful thing to have happened. She looked at the old woman on the bed and she thought she saw just the faintest gleam of something in her eye, as if she, too, thought it was funny. But she could have been imagining it.

"Tell her about the sheep-shearing," Anne suggested, when Kate had got to the end of her tale of woe.

Kate carried on talking. She described how Siobhan had called for her, how Michael had let her have a go at shearing, how the dogs had obeyed Liam's whistles, how she had seen the puppies and how adorable they were. She didn't say that she had also thought Liam was rather good-looking.

After a little while her grandmother's eyes closed and she fell asleep. Anne stood up. "Time for us to go," she said.

On the way back to the car park she said, "You were very good."

"Was I?"

"Yes. It isn't easy. I find I run out of things to say very quickly, but you managed to keep on talking."

"Do you think it did any good?" Kate asked.

"I would have thought it was bound to."

That afternoon Siobhan turned up again, as she had promised. The two girls decided to make the journey up to the turf bog.

"Are you sure that's what you want to do?" Siobhan asked. Kate had told her how it had gone so disastrously wrong the first time.

"I'm not going to let it beat me," Kate said.

"If you carry on along the path that leads to the turf bog it will bring you to the river," Anne told them.

"Is there a river on the land?" Kate asked.

"It's only a stream, really," Anne said. "But it's nice when it's in flood."

It was a beautiful day outside. The sun was shining but the air was fresh. A blue sky was full of little puffy clouds. You felt that it could rain if it wanted to, but if you were lucky, it just might not. "I thought it was supposed to rain here all the time," Kate said.

"Who told you that?" Siobhan asked.

"My mother."

"Well," Siobhan said. "Maybe it does rain a bit, but not all the time. It's soft weather we have here."

"Soft weather?" Kate said.

"That's what the old people call it," Siobhan explained. "It means moist, you know. It's what keeps the place green. You have heatwaves in London, don't you?"

The last two summers in London had been incredibly hot. On the television they had said that it was a record.

"London's not particularly nice in the heat," Kate said. "It gets gritty and full of exhaust fumes."

"Do you go out much?" Siobhan asked.

"How do you mean?"

"Oh, you know, parties, discos, clubs."

"Not much," Kate asked. She went to a few parties but discos weren't really her thing. As for clubs – there was no way that Anne would let her go to West End nightclubs.

"There's a festival on in Cruachan next week, did you know?" Siobhan said.

"What sort of festival?" Kate asked.

"A village festival."

"Will it be good?"

Siobhan shrugged. "It won't be anything like London," she said.

Kate ignored this remark. She was getting tired of this constant comparison of everything to London. "What sort of things will there be?"

"Everything," Siobhan said. "There's concerts, discos, competitions. It's great craic."

"It's what?"

Siobhan laughed. "Have you not heard that?" she asked. "Great craic. It's what we say over here. It means good fun."

"Oh, I see."

They had been climbing the path for some time now and they began at last to see ahead of them, a red five-bar gate that blocked the path. "There's the gate," Kate said. "There should be a gap in the hedge on the left."

Sure enough, just in front of the gate, there was an opening in the hedge which led on to the open moorland that lay on that side of the path. As far as the eye could see there was heather and grass. A small, almost entirely overgrown path led from the opening across the heather. Halfway along the path a huge grey rock stuck out from the ground, like a weird piece of sculpture.

"This must be the path to the turf bog," Kate said.

"No one's been along this for a long time," Siobhan said. "Come on."

The ground under their feet was springy, as if they were walking on foam rubber. The grass grew in tussocks. Moss was everywhere in between, and out of the moss grew heather, its little purple flowers looking like bells. A keen wind rushed towards them as soon as they left the shelter of the path, making conversation difficult.

After a while they found themselves on a bank. The ground on one side had been cut away to a depth of about six feet. Pools of water covered it in places. In other parts, the bare black earth showed through.

"This is the turf bog," Siobhan said. "That's how they cut it. One man stands down there, cuts the turves and throws them up to someone up here."

Kate and Siobhan stood on the rim of the turf bog, staring down at the puddles of brackish water below. Kate remembered Anne's description of how she had stood where Kate was standing now and watched her grandfather cut turf. It occurred to her that her mother's childhood had been very unlike her own. She felt a stab of something which she realised must be envy.

The wind that had been singing in their ears all the way up the hill was lulled. Kate turned slowly round in a full circle. There was nothing but green in all directions, stretching all the way to the dark blue mountains that stood out against the sky. For a moment it seemed to Kate that the whole countryside was asleep and dreaming of another time. No, that was not right. She felt as if she, herself, with her memories of London, the café and the school term that had just finished, was the dream. This was real.

They walked across the rim of the bog to the rock they had seen from the path. It was bigger than both of them and almost square. One side of it was propped on top of another huge slab and to look at it you might have expected that you could push it over with your hands. But that was only the way it looked. You would need giant hands to move these stones.

Kate stood close to the rock and stared at the surface of it. Lichen and moss had grown on it and died leaving yellow, white and even purple stains, and there were patterns of tiny holes that must have been left by the roots of plants long since dead.

"It's like a map," Kate said. "Or like some sort of mysterious writing."

Siobhan examined the rock. "So it is," she said. "Do you know last night there was something tapping at my window all night."

"What do you mean?" Kate asked her.

"I kept hearing someone tapping at the window. I told my aunt about it and she said it was probably just a branch, but it didn't sound like that to me."

Kate thought about this. "I expect it *was* a branch," she said.

Siobhan looked disappointed.

"You just have a vivid imagination," Kate told her.

"That's what my mother's always saying," Siobhan complained. "Do you believe in ghosts?"

Kate shook her head. "I don't think so."

"I do," Siobhan told her.

"Have you ever seen one?"

"No," she admitted. "Not yet, anyway."

Kate smiled. She liked the way that nothing daunted Siobhan for very long.

"Do you ever wake up in the night with the feeling that there was someone standing there just a few moments earlier?"

"No I don't," Kate said. "That sounds really frightening. Is that what happens to you?"

Siobhan shook her head. "No," she said, "but I read about it in a magazine."

Kate laughed. "I thought you were serious for a minute," she said.

"It's true, though," Siobhan said. "At least the magazine said it was true."

"On my first morning here," Kate said. "I woke up

and I realised that I had no idea where I was."

"I do that all the time," Siobhan said.

"Honestly, Siobhan," Kate said. "You are bonkers."

"Am I?" Siobhan looked hurt.

"I didn't mean it like that," Kate said, suddenly wishing she hadn't said it, but Siobhan's face broke into a broad grin. "Maybe I am," she said. She walked around the rock to the other side and Kate followed her. A clump of gorse grew at its base. Kate bent down to admire its prickly leaves that stood up like little spears. "Do you know what my teacher at school said about me?" she said, standing up.

"What?"

"He said that I had absolutely no imagination."

"That wasn't very nice," Siobhan said.

"He's not a very nice man. At least ... you know what school is like," she added.

Siobhan nodded. That was one thing that was probably the same all over the world, Kate reflected.

"I used to believe it as well," Kate said. "I used to walk around thinking, 'I've got no imagination.' I've just realised it isn't true."

"What changed your mind?" Siobhan asked her.

Kate stretched her hand out to include the whole countryside. "Seeing this. It's so beautiful," she said.

"Do you think so?" Siobhan asked. She seemed to be looking at Kate carefully.

"Of course I do," Kate said. "Anyone can see it's beautiful."

"Not as exciting as London, though," Siobhan suggested.

"Why do you keep going on about London?" Kate asked her.

"It's where everyone goes," Siobhan said. "Dublin, London, Europe and America."

"But why?" Kate asked.

Siobhan shrugged. "Jobs, I suppose."

"Will you leave?" Kate asked.

"I don't know," Siobhan said. "I've a few years before I have to decide."

"If I lived here I wouldn't leave," Kate said suddenly. She hadn't meant to say it. It just popped out.

"But if you lived here, you wouldn't be you," said Siobhan, "if you see what I mean. Come on, let's see if we can find the river."

They left the path and began walking on the thick heather, grass and moss that gave way beneath their feet like a sort of mattress.

"Michael isn't leaving, is he?" Kate asked, as they walked along.

"No. He's staying. Everyone knows that."

Kate wondered about his brother Liam. What would he do when his turn came?

The land began to slope downwards towards the river and they had to concentrate now to keep their balance. "There must be so much to do in London," Siobhan said. "I read somewhere that there are restaurants serving food from every country in the world in London."

"I suppose there are," agreed Kate.

"And there are clubs and cinemas and shops."

"But there isn't this," Kate said. She stopped and listened. There was no sound at all, just the wind, the birds and somewhere in the distance the faint noise of the river. "I love it here," she said. She realised that she really meant it.

"Do you honestly?" Siobhan asked her.

"Of course."

"Promise you're not joking?"

Kate looked at her in surprise. "Why would I be joking?" she asked.

"I don't know," Siobhan said. "I just wanted to make sure."

They walked on in silence. Kate had a feeling that she had just passed some sort of test.

"I love it too," Siobhan said, after a long pause. "It's the best place in the world."

That evening, after Siobhan had gone home, Anne and Kate sat watching the television. There wasn't much on but Kate didn't mind. She was tired after her walk up to the turf bog, but it was a nice kind of tiredness. She wondered idly how many days they had been in

Ireland. They had left on the Tuesday morning and spent most of the day travelling. On Wednesday she had gone exploring with disastrous consequences. On Thursday Siobhan had come round and they had gone to the sheep-shearing. With today, that made four days. Only four – it seemed much longer.

If she had told her friends at school that she had gone to a sheep-shearing and that she had really enjoyed it, they would probably have laughed at her. They would have made jokes about her, calling her things like 'Farmer Kate'. She could just hear them. But it was true, all the same. There was something about it that seemed more real than most of the things that happened to her. Of course part of the reason for that was Liam. He was nice. Her friend Emma would have said that he was 'cute' or maybe 'sweet'. All boys worth considering were either cute or sweet to her. But Kate did not want to fit Liam into one of these categories. He was different from the boys they talked about back in England. That was what she liked about him.

She knew what she had to do and even though there was no one to see here, she felt embarrassed about it. But she was going through with it anyway. She got up, went into the kitchen, opened the door of the refrigerator and got out the milk. She poured some into a glass and drank it in one long gulp, then, speaking very softly, in case Anne heard her, she said, "Liam, Liam, Liam, Liam, Liam." Then she put the bottle of milk back in the fridge, rinsed the glass and put it on the draining board. She went back into the living room.

"Everything all right?" Anne asked, without taking her eyes away from the television screen.

"Fine," Kate said. She sat back down again and carried on watching TV.

Chapter Ten

"You don't have to come every day, you know," Anne said on the way to the hospital the following morning.

"I know that," Kate replied.

"It can't be very interesting for you."

"It's all right, honest."

Anne took Kate's hand and squeezed it. "Thank you for being so understanding," she said.

"That's OK," Kate said, but she couldn't help feeling that she wasn't actually being understanding. She didn't really understand Anne's feelings. But then she never did. Anne kept them under lock and key. Perhaps she was just being curious. She just didn't want anything else to happen in her family that she didn't see. She wanted to make sure that she was involved, whether Anne wanted her to be or not.

"What will happen to Grandma if the land is sold?" Kate asked.

"I don't know," Anne said.

"Where would she live?"

"She may not come out of hospital again, Kate."

"But she is beginning to make a recovery, isn't she?"

"Yes," Anne agreed. "But how much is she going to recover? We just don't know."

"So you are going to do what Dennis Carthy wants?"

"I don't know," Anne said. "I told you, I'm thinking about it. But someone has to look after the farm and it can't be me."

"Why not?"

"Kate, you can't run a farm in Ireland from a café in London."

"But does it take much running? Surely the land just looks after itself?"

Anne turned to look at her in surprise. Then she turned back to concentrate on the road ahead. "You're very interested all of a sudden," she said.

"Well, I'm here, aren't I? You brought me to Ireland with you," Kate said. "Anyway ..."

"Anyway what?"

"Oh nothing." Kate had been about to say, "Anyway, I have a right to be interested," but she wasn't sure if that was true. The truth was that she wasn't sure why she was so interested herself. She just had a feeling that something important was happening

111

and she didn't want Anne to get it wrong.

Kate's grandmother was propped up on pillows when they arrived. "Well," Anne said with determined cheeriness, "look at you."

The nurse came into the room. "She's making great progress," she told them. "Aren't you, dear?" she added, turning to Nora.

There was a moment's pause while the nurse, Anne and Kate all looked expectantly at Kate's grandmother, and then she gave a very faint nod of her head.

"Now," the nurse said. "Will you look at that?" She spoke as if her patient had flung off her blankets, climbed out of bed and danced a jig in front of them. "I'll leave you three together then," she added, disappearing out of the door.

Anne and Kate sat down on either side of the bed. "Here we are again," Anne said. She looked at Nora and Nora looked back at her. Then there was silence.

Suddenly Kate found herself speaking, partly to fill the silence and partly because she wanted to speak to her grandmother. "Did you really have a donkey?" she said.

Her grandmother's eyes swivelled from Anne's face to Kate's. Again came that barely perceptible nod.

"I wish I did," Kate said. "They've got such lovely faces."

"Pity they've got such stubborn natures, then, isn't it?" Anne said.

"Are they really stubborn?" Kate asked.

"They certainly are," Anne said. "They only do what *they* want to do, not what you want them to do."

"I can think of some people who are like that," Kate said. She hadn't really meant to say it out loud because of course she was thinking about Anne, but it just came out.

Her grandmother's eyes again flicked from Anne's face to Kate's face and – was Kate imagining it, or did the ghost of a smile pass across the old woman's face?

"I went all the way up to the turf bog yesterday," Kate went on. "Siobhan and I went together. It's really beautiful up there." She described the rock with the marks that the lichen had made and how she had thought it looked like writing.

"I used to sit with my back against that rock," Anne said, "while my dad cut turf."

Kate wanted to say, "How could you have left it all behind?" but she didn't because she remembered that all the reasons why Anne had left it behind were gathered together in that room: Kate herself and her grandmother's disapproval. She should have felt angry at the old woman. Whenever she had thought about what it would be like meeting her grandmother, and she had thought about it a great deal on the journey from London, she had felt anger against this person she

113

had never met for her stupid, prejudiced ways, but strangely, sitting here beside her bed, she felt only sadness. She felt as if she had missed out on something, but that the loss was not just hers. They had all missed out on something.

After a little while her grandmother began to get tired. Her eyes shut and opened, then shut again.

"We'll leave you to get some sleep," Anne said. "I'll be back tomorrow."

"So will I," Kate added.

They started to stand up to leave, but the old woman's eyes flicked open again. She looked intently at Kate. It seemed to Kate that she was very anxious to say something, but found it terribly hard to speak. Ever so slowly she opened her mouth. She was clearly struggling to say something. She began to shake with the effort.

"It's all right, Mother," Anne said. "Don't strain yourself."

But her mother ignored her. She fixed her eyes on Kate's eyes. Her lips quivered and a sound came out of her. "H ... h."

"What is it?" Kate asked, bending her ear to her grandmother's mouth.

"Home," she said at last in a barely audible whisper.

"Home?" Kate said.

Her grandmother gave the faintest of nods, then she

sank down on to the pillows in exhaustion. Just at that point the nurse returned. "Well now, you've had a nice long visit," she said, sweeping in briskly with a thermometer in her hand.

"She spoke," Kate said.

"Did she now?" said the nurse. "Well that's very good. You're doing awfully well," she went on, looking at Nora. She reminded Kate of a teacher she had at primary school. She was nice, but she did talk to everyone as if they were about five years old, even the parents.

Afterwards, in the corridor, Kate said, "What do you think she meant?"

"She wants us to take her home, I expect," Anne said.

But Kate did not think this was what her grandmother had meant at all. She had looked particularly at herself, not at Anne. If she had wanted to be taken home, surely she would have said that to Anne. No, Kate was sure that the old woman wanted to say, "Welcome home." Of course she had no proof, nothing except a feeling. Just before her grandmother had actually spoken, Kate had been certain that was what she was going to say. She decided not to tell this to Anne. Kate wasn't sure why not; perhaps just because Anne knew Kate's grandmother and she herself did not.

Chapter Eleven

"WE'RE GOING to have a bonfire." Those were the words with which Siobhan greeted Kate the next morning when she arrived just after breakfast.

"Who is?" Kate asked her.

"Everyone," Siobhan said. "All the young people round here. Michael will be there and Liam."

"And his friend Sean?" Kate said teasingly as she began to guess the reason for Siobhan's excitement.

"Sean too," Siobhan said. "It'll be great craic."

"Great craic," Kate repeated after her, amused at the expression.

"That's it," Siobhan said. "You're learning."

"When will it be and where?"

"Tonight at the Dooleys', where the sheep-shearing was," Siobhan told her.

"Who else will come?" Kate wanted to know.

"Oh everyone," Siobhan said, reeling off a list of names that meant nothing to Kate. "You'll get to meet them all. You'll like them."

Kate wondered whether she would. She hoped so.

"We'll need some food," Siobhan said.

"We could have marshmallows," Kate said, "toasted in the bonfire." She had eaten these at a bonfire party many years ago but she still remembered the experience.

"We'll need to go into Cruachan," Siobhan said.

"You can come with me," Anne told them.

They bought the marshmallows in the same shop that Anne and Kate had gone to on their first morning. They also bought apples, crisps, bread for toasting and cocoa.

"Marshmallows are good floating on the top of cocoa, too," Siobhan said. "You wait until you try them."

After she had dropped them off at the shop, Anne went to the hospital. Siobhan had promised to show Kate the community centre.

"What's it like?" Kate asked as they walked from the shop.

"It's nice," Siobhan said. "It used to be just a church hall when your mother lived here, but now it's all done up."

In the community centre there was a modern drama studio. "That's where they have the concerts when the festival is on," Siobhan said. There was also a café, two pool tables and a table-tennis room. Siobhan headed straight for one of the pool tables where Liam and another boy, whom Kate did not recognise but guessed must be Sean, were playing.

It was Liam's shot. He looked up and groaned as they came over.

"That's not fair," he said. "I'll never get it now."

"Surely you're not put off by an audience," Siobhan said.

"I can't play when people are watching me," he said, but he bent down again and took aim with his cue. He struck the white ball with the tip of the cue. It went exactly where he intended, knocking his own ball into the corner pocket.

"That wasn't bad, for someone who can't play in front of an audience," the other boy said.

"This is Sean," Siobhan said to Kate. "This is Kate," she told Sean.

He smiled at her. He was taller than Liam and quite good-looking, but she preferred Liam.

"You're the girl from London," Sean said.

"That's me," Kate said. "And before you say it must be great living in London, it isn't, at least not particularly."

Sean looked puzzled. "I wasn't going to say that at all," he protested. "I was only going to ask you ..."

"How I like Ireland," Kate finished for him. "That's the other thing people keep saying to me and the answer is, I like it a lot."

"That's the end of that conversation then," Sean said.

"It's your turn anyway," Liam told him. He had just missed his next shot, even though this time no one had been watching.

Sean picked up his cue, which had been leaning against the wall, and bent over the table.

"How are the puppies?" Kate asked Liam

"Wandering about and falling over each other," Liam said. "Are you coming to the bonfire?"

"We've just been buying food for it," she told him.

"Sean and myself have collected a stack of wood for it," Liam said.

"Have you?"

"We have. Kieran Rooney and Jimmy Gilbride helped. We spent two hours at it last night."

"We should have enough wood then," Kate said. It wasn't a very exciting thing to say, she knew that, but she wanted to keep the conversation going.

"It burns very quickly," Liam told her. She sensed that he, too, wanted to keep talking and that for him as well it was an effort to overcome shyness.

"Do you often have bonfires?" she asked. Everything she said sounded so ridiculous, so forced, but it didn't matter.

"Not that often," Liam said.

"Not that often?" chipped in Siobhan who had

been standing by the pool table watching Sean play. "When was the last time we had a bonfire around here?"

Liam shrugged.

"We never have bonfires," Siobhan said. "Liam has organised this one entirely in your honour," she told Kate. She turned to Liam. "Isn't that right?" she asked him, teasingly.

Liam blushed and looked at the floor. Kate felt sorry for him. "Thank you," she said.

"Your shot, Liam," Sean said, coming over to join them.

"I thought you were going to be at the sheep-shearing," Siobhan said to Sean.

"I had to work," he said. "My father wanted me to give him a hand with a bit of fencing."

Just from the way he spoke, Kate sensed that he was not quite as keen as Siobhan was. She felt sorry for her friend.

"That's it," Liam announced. "I've missed again. You can clear up now." He meant that he had effectively lost the game, and within a few minutes Sean announced that he had won.

"Do you fancy a game?" Liam asked Kate suddenly.

"I can't play," she said. It was the truth, though she wished she hadn't said it as soon as the words were out of her mouth.

"It's easy. I'll show you." He looked at her expectantly. "If you like, that is," he added, suddenly losing confidence.

"That'd be great," she said.

Liam looked delighted.

"You can have this," Sean said, handing her his cue. "I'm going to get something to drink." He wandered over to the café with Siobhan in tow.

Liam set the balls up in a triangle in the middle of the table. "Do you know how to hold the cue?" he asked.

"Like this?" she said, holding it as she had seen snooker players do on the television.

"That's perfect," Liam said.

For a moment Kate felt slightly disappointed. She had wanted him to come over and hold the cue with her, as his brother Michael had done with the shears. But Liam was too shy for that.

"You go first," he said. "Just aim to break up the pack."

Kate was hopeless. Her first shot missed the pack altogether and even when Liam insisted that was only a practice shot and let her try again, she only caught the white ball a glancing blow with the tip of her cue and sent it rolling feebly into the pack. In front of anyone else she would have been embarrassed, but Liam just smiled.

"It takes a while to get your eye in," he told her.

By the end of the game she was getting the ball to go where she wanted it to and she did actually get some balls in. Every time she did, Liam said, "Well done," as if he really meant it.

After they had finished, Siobhan and Sean played a game. Siobhan was good but not quite as good as Sean, who, Kate couldn't help feeling, fancied himself just a little bit too much.

Anne had arranged to meet them outside in an hour and it was surprising how quickly the time passed. Kate felt a bit like Cinderella when she looked at her watch and suddenly realised it was time to go.

"Mum will be waiting," she told Siobhan.

"OK," Siobhan said. "We'll see you two tonight."

Liam looked straight into Kate's eyes. "See you," he said.

"See you," Kate said.

On the way out, Siobhan said, "You've certainly made a hit with Liam."

"Have I?" Kate said.

"*Have I?*" said Siobhan. "Listen to little Miss Innocent."

Kate turned to look at her. Was Siobhan criticising her? But the look on Siobhan's face was friendly, though teasing.

"What's the poster for?" Kate said, to change the subject. A brightly coloured poster was pinned up just inside the door.

"Something to do with the festival," Siobhan told her.

Kate stopped to read the poster. "Traditional Music Seisun," it read. "August 4th."

"That's a funny way to spell 'session'," Kate said.

"It's Irish," Siobhan said. "Come on, it's only a traditional music concert. You don't want to know about that."

"But I do," Kate protested. "I like traditional Irish music." It was true. She had heard Irish jigs and reels before and she had liked the wildness of them.

"There'll be discos," Siobhan said. "They'll be more fun."

"I just want to see what it says," Kate insisted. She carried on reading, "An evening of musical magic with Cruachan's own Joe Hendry plus supporting acts." She stopped dead. "Cruachan's own Joe Hendry." It couldn't be, could it?

"Are you coming?" Siobhan asked.

"What?"

"Your mother will be waiting."

Kate looked at her and wondered: did Siobhan know something she did not? "Siobhan?" she began.

"Yes."

Siobhan's expression was perfectly innocent. Kate decided that she was just being ridiculous. "Nothing," she said. She turned from the poster and walked out of the community centre.

Outside Anne was sitting in the car, waiting. "Did you have a nice time?" she asked.

"Yes thanks," Kate replied. She said nothing else all the way back home. It didn't matter because Siobhan was happy to chat away. She showed Anne the things they had bought and told her about the community centre and about Kate playing pool.

After they had dropped Siobhan off at the bottom of the land which led to her aunt's farm, Anne said, "You're very quiet, Kate."

"I'm just a bit tired," Kate said.

"Probably a delayed reaction to the journey," Anne said. "I expect it's all catching up with you now. Do you think you'll be all right for this bonfire, tonight?"

"I expect so," Kate said absent-mindedly. Then she added, "Are you going to the festival?"

"What festival?" Anne asked her.

"In Cruachan."

"I didn't know there was one," Anne said.

"Siobhan says they have one every year," Kate insisted.

"Well that must have started after I left," Anne said. She did not sound interested.

"There's concerts and discos and other things," Kate went on.

"That's nice."

"Don't you want to go to any of them?"

"Oh, Kate," Anne said, "I really don't want to get

involved in anything like that. I've got too much on my mind. You go to anything you like. You don't need me to go with you, do you?"

"No," Kate said.

"I mean I hardly think I'd fit in at a disco," Anne went on, smiling at the picture of herself she had created.

"There are other things."

"I know," Anne said, "but I think I'll give it a miss." The way she said it made it clear that she wasn't interested in talking about it any further. Instead she said, "I do hope everything is all right in the café."

"Why shouldn't it be?" Kate said.

"I told Marian to phone me last night, that's all," Anne said.

"Perhaps she forgot," Kate suggested.

"I don't pay her to forget," Anne said tersely.

When they got home Anne went straight inside and telephoned the café. Kate could hear her telling Marian off. "You should have carried on trying," she said. On the whole Anne was a kind and considerate employer, but she could be tough when she wanted to. Kate listened to the conversation for a while, then she went upstairs and lay down on her bed. The same thoughts went round and round in her head. Was it him? If it was, did Anne know about the concert? She decided that the answer to the second question was probably no. But what about the answer to the first?

After a while, Anne put the telephone down and Kate could hear her clattering around in the kitchen. Just from the noise she made, Kate could tell that she was not in a good mood. When Anne was angry she didn't shout or swear, but she did shut cupboard doors very loudly and bang down cups and plates on the table. After a while she called upstairs, "Do you want a cup of tea?"

"Yes please," Kate called back.

When Anne came up five minutes later with two cups of tea and sat on the end of the bed drinking hers, Kate asked her, "How was Marian?"

"Marian was Marian," Anne said, as if that was explanation enough.

"Is everything all right?" Kate asked her.

"No."

"What's the matter?"

"The drains are blocked."

"Oh."

"Honestly," Anne said, as if she were talking to Marian all over again. "You wouldn't think it would be impossible just to open the Yellow Pages, find a plumber and give him a ring, would you?"

"Didn't Marian do that?"

"She said she was having trouble. Apparently she phoned someone and he said he was coming and then he didn't turn up and she phoned someone else and he said he couldn't come until the end of the week and then she phoned someone else and all she got was an ansaphone."

"Perhaps there are a lot of emergencies going on," Kate suggested.

Anne didn't look as if she thought much of this remark. "Perhaps Marian isn't quite as competent as I thought she was," she replied.

"I'm sure that isn't true," Kate said. "She's probably doing her best."

"Yes, well, it isn't good enough," Anne said. "First she forgets to phone me. Then she tells me she can't find a plumber. In the middle of London. For God's sake!" She shook her head in despair and sipped her tea. "I think I'm going to have to look into Mr Carthy's suggestion a bit more carefully."

"You mean about getting – what was it?"

"Power of attorney."

"Yes. But surely Grandma is getting better. I mean, she spoke yesterday."

"That's true," Anne said. "But it's going to take weeks, months more likely, and I haven't got that time. I've got a business to run."

"You're going to sell the land then?" Kate said. It sounded terrible when she said it, like a death sentence being pronounced on the place.

"I haven't decided anything yet."

They both sat in silence drinking their tea. Then Kate spoke. "Mum," she said.

"Yes."

"About my father?"

"What about him?" Anne said stiffly.

"Do you think he still works as a musician?"

"Now how would I know the answer to that, Kate?" Anne replied.

"But what do you think?"

"I don't know. The last thing I heard about him he was playing in a bar in Dublin. So maybe." She stood up. "I've just remembered that plumber we got in when the central heating went. He was tremendous. I must go and phone Marian."

Chapter Twelve

SIOBHAN CALLED for Kate that evening. It was already quite dark as they walked up the road to where the bonfire was being held.

"Be careful of cars," Anne had told Kate time and time again.

"I will, Mum," Kate said.

"It's not like in London," Anne went on. "There are no street lights and drivers can't see you until they're right on top of you."

"Siobhan's got a torch."

"All the same."

"I'll be careful. I promise."

Once outside, Kate could understand her mother's anxiety. It was completely dark, except for the light of the moon and stars. "I've never gone out at night like this," she told Siobhan.

"What do you mean?"

"With everything so dark."

"You soon get used to it," Siobhan said. But Kate

didn't think she would ever get used to this. It seemed so utterly magical. Suddenly they heard a wild shrieking noise that made Kate stop in her tracks. "What was that?" she demanded. It had sounded like someone being murdered.

"A fox," Siobhan said. She shone her torch in an arc over the fields on the side from which the cry had come. "I can't see it," she said. "Sometimes you can catch their eyes in the light, but it was too far away."

"It sounded almost human."

"They do," Siobhan said. "I thought you got them in London."

"We do," Kate said. "But I've never heard one close up like that."

They carried on walking in the darkness. After a while Kate's eyes adjusted and she could make out much more around her.

"Did you ever hear about the banshee?" Siobhan asked.

"The what?"

"The banshee."

"No."

"It means the woman of the hills," Siobhan told her. "She is supposed to follow certain families around and you can hear her crying in the night just before someone in that family is going to die."

Kate felt goose pimples starting up all over her body.

"Do you believe in it?"

"Sometimes," Siobhan said. "But other times I think it's just what people said when they heard noises like that. My grandmother swears that it's true."

"You can see why," Kate said. She meant that if you took away some of the modern things, like the tarmac on the road, and Siobhan's electric torch, you could believe that anything might be true.

"What did you think of Sean?" Siobhan asked.

Kate smiled. She was amused at the way Siobhan's mood changed from the fantastic to the down-to-earth in a moment. "He seemed nice," she said diplomatically.

"He *is* nice," Siobhan said. Even in the darkness Kate could see that a big smile was creeping over Siobhan's face. She turned and caught Kate looking at her. "Well," she said. "I think he is."

"I didn't disagree with you," Kate protested, laughing.

"I think he's gorgeous," said Siobhan. A full moon came out from behind a cloud and lit up the way before them. "I bet Liam asks you to the disco," she went on.

"Do you think he will?"

"I'm sure of it. What will you say?"

"I don't know," Kate said. "Yes, I suppose."

"If Sean asks me, I'm going to say yes," Siobhan said.

"Do you think he will?"

"He'd better," Siobhan said. "If he doesn't, I'll ask him."

"Do you have to go to the disco with someone?" Kate said. "Can't you just go on your own?"

"You can, of course," Siobhan said. "Everyone goes together anyway. But you can be with someone as well."

They turned down the lane that led to the Dooleys' farm, where the bonfire was being held.

You could hear and see the bonfire from some way off. Its fierce red top was visible dancing above the hedges on either side of the lane, throwing up showers of sparks. And you could hear the noise of it, a subdued roaring, like the sound of some gigantic cat, and on top of that, a crackling. Then they came round the corner and there it was in front of them.

"It's huge!" Kate exclaimed.

It *was* huge. Liam and his friends had taken the business of getting wood very seriously. The fierce red tongue of flame licked furiously against the black sky. You could feel the heat thrusting out of it from some distance away.

"It's not bad at all," Siobhan said. The two girls stood there looking at the bonfire. Young people were standing around in groups. The faces that were turned to the fire were lit up with an orange glow. Those that were turned away were in complete shadow. One of the group detached itself from the others and came over to meet them. It was Liam. "I'm glad you could come," he said to them both.

"It's a brilliant bonfire," Kate told him.

"It's a bit mad," Liam said. "But Michael's got the hose connected, just in case. Have you brought the food?"

Siobhan held up the plastic bag that she had been carrying. "It's all here," she told him.

"That's great," he said. "Bring it over to the table."

They put the food on a table on which other food and drinks had been placed. Sean came over to join them. "How's the Londoner?" he asked Kate.

She couldn't help it – he annoyed her a little bit. Just something about his manner. But he meant well and Siobhan liked him.

"I'm OK," she said.

"Do you go out much in the evening over in London?" he asked.

"A bit," Kate said.

"What kind of music do you like?"

Kate began listing the names of some of the groups she liked. Sean shook his head. He either hadn't heard of them or didn't like them. But Liam smiled at every name. "They're good," he said, and, "They're good too."

"You haven't heard of half of them," Sean said.

"Yes I have," Liam told him. "Sean is a musical dunce," he said.

"Better than being an actual dunce," Sean said. It was good-humoured banter but Kate wondered if there wasn't a slight edge to it.

"Liam Dooley you are the stupidest boy I have ever met," Sean said, putting on a silly voice. Siobhan giggled.

"Who's that meant to be?" Kate asked.

"Our old teacher, Mrs Riley," Liam told her. "Moaning Riley, they call her. She hated me. Every time she saw me she used to find something to tell me off about."

"I know the feeling," Kate said, thinking of the teacher who had told her she had no imagination.

Some of the others now came over to join them and Kate was introduced to boys and girls in turn and mixed up their names almost immediately. She talked to them all. Everyone was friendly, made jokes, told her about themselves and asked her questions about herself. She was pretty sure that there was no one there she didn't speak to.

After a while she found herself talking to Liam on his own again. "Are you going ...?" he started to say and then he stopped again and looked at the ground. Kate waited for him to carry on but he didn't.

"What did you say?" she asked.

"Oh nothing," he mumbled.

"You were going to ask me if I was going somewhere," Kate said, trying to help him.

"Oh yeah," Liam said, acting as if he had just remembered. "I was just wondering if you were going to any of the festival events."

"I might be," Kate said.

"There's a traditional music session first," he said.

"I know," Kate said, her voice was very carefully neutral. She hadn't expected this. She had thought that he was going to ask her about the disco.

"I'm helping my brother with the PA," he said.

"The PA?"

"Public address. You know, mikes, loudspeakers."

"Oh, right."

"I wondered if you fancied coming along."

"Me?" She didn't want to sound discouraging, but she couldn't help herself. All afternoon she had been thinking about it and she had made up her mind that she was going to go, but on her own. She hadn't wanted other people to be there with her.

"I know it isn't your kind of music," he went on, beginning to stutter slightly as he realised the suggestion was not going well.

"No, I like it," Kate said. "Irish music, I mean. I do like it, what I've heard. I just thought you were going to say something else."

"What?" Liam said, looking confused.

"It doesn't matter," Kate said.

They stood looking at each other. The whole thing was suddenly going very badly wrong.

Kate decided to tell him that she had thought he was going to ask her about the disco. She opened her mouth to speak, when Siobhan and Sean materialised at her side. "So this is where you are," Siobhan said. She had a pleased look on her face.

"When are we going to have the food?" Sean asked.

"Let's have some now," Liam said. He went over to the table and busied himself opening some giant bags of crisps.

"Sean asked me to the disco," Siobhan said when they were alone together.

"Good," Kate replied.

"Did Liam say anything?" she asked.

"Not about the disco," Kate said.

For the rest of the night Kate kept hoping she would get a chance to speak to Liam on his own, but the opportunity didn't arise. He avoided being on his own with her. She must have offended him, she realised.

They ate all the food, and drank cocoa with marshmallows melted on the top. Siobhan was right: it did taste delicious, but Kate didn't really care; she just wanted to put things right with Liam.

After the fire had died down and was just a great heap of glowing embers, they speared more marshmallows on long sticks and toasted them. They were burnt black on the outside but melted inside.

Kate looked at her watch. She realised that they would have to leave quite soon. Anne had been very firm about what time she wanted Kate back, and she was always very precise about things like that.

At last she saw Liam standing on the other side of the bonfire, on his own. Kate quickly walked over to him. She had decided what she wanted to say.

"Liam," she said.

He looked up uncertainly.

"I just wanted to say I would like to come to the concert with you."

"Would you?" His face broke out into a wide grin.

"Yes I would." She had no idea how she was going to handle this but she had decided one thing: she did not want to disappoint him; he was too nice.

"I've got to go now," she told him. "I'll see you on the fourth."

"Right."

"That's the day after tomorrow, isn't it?"

"Yes," he said. "I'll call for you."

"OK."

They stood looking at each other, both smiling. Neither seemed to be able to turn and leave. "Right then," Kate said.

"Right."

"See you then."

"OK."

Kate turned round and walked back to Siobhan.

"You look pleased with yourself," Siobhan said.

"Do I?" Kate said.

"You look like a cat that's been at the cream," Siobhan told her.

But only part of Kate felt like that. Underneath, in a deeper part of her, there was nothing but unanswered questions and uncertain feelings.

Chapter Thirteen

THE NEXT morning Kate woke up with the same two thoughts in her mind: Liam and the concert. She wished she had someone to talk it over with, but there was no one. On the way back, Siobhan had asked her what she had said to Liam and she had told her, but she couldn't tell her the whole story and she certainly didn't want to tell Anne.

"I'm going in to Cruachan to see a solicitor this morning," Anne announced over the breakfast table.

"A solicitor. Why?"

"Just to get the answers to a few questions." That was typical of Anne. She never gave away any information unless she had to, but Kate knew what it meant: Anne had decided to begin the process which would end with the sale of the land to Dennis Carthy. With this conviction came an equally certain feeling that she did not want the land sold. She could not have said exactly why, but she knew that she did not.

"Are you sure that's a good idea?"

Anne looked at Kate in surprise. She didn't like having her decisions challenged. She thought about things for a long time, then she made up her mind, usually without reference to anyone else, certainly not to Kate. "I told you," she said, "I'm just finding out information." But Kate knew her better. She knew what her mother was like.

"I'll come in with you," Kate said, "and visit Grandma."

"If you like," Anne said.

They drove into the hospital car park together and then Anne went off to see the solicitor. "I'll meet you back here at eleven o'clock," she said.

Kate made her own way into the hospital and along the dreary chemical-smelling corridors to the room where her grandmother was.

Nora was awake. She looked up as Kate went into the room and smiled with half of her face. The other half, the doctor had told them, had been paralysed by the stroke, although there was some possibility that she might regain control over it.

"The brain is an extraordinary organ," he had told Anne and Kate. "Sometimes you can damage large parts of it, but what remains can somehow learn to carry on just as before. Other times, you knock out a tiny area and the patient remains like a vegetable."

That was a horrible expression, 'like a vegetable', and the easy way in which the doctor had said it had made Kate shudder. Her grandmother was certainly not like a vegetable. The eyes that she turned on Kate seemed full of expectation. It was that look, which seemed so eager to communicate, that decided Kate. She would go through with the plan that had been forming in her mind ever since Anne's announcement at the breakfast table. She sat down beside the bed.

"It's me, Kate," she said. "Remember me?"

Nora nodded.

"Of course you do. I want to tell you something. It's important. Do you understand?"

Again, Nora nodded.

"You've got to get better, quickly, otherwise Anne will have to sell the land."

The old woman's face looked shocked. "She doesn't want to," Kate said, quickly, "but she's got a café to run in London."

Nora looked hopelessly confused. "Anne runs a café in London, didn't you know that?" Kate asked. "She owns it. It's her own business. It's a really good café. It's really a bistro, like a little restaurant. People bring their own wine because it's not licensed."

Nora still looked confused.

"Oh dear," Kate said. "I'm not doing this very well. Look, Anne will have to go back to England soon. She can't stay here for ever and when she does, who will look after the land? That's why you have to get better."

Even as she said it, it occurred to Kate that the idea of

this fragile old woman looking after anything was a fairly unlikely one. She was clearly quite incapable of looking after herself at the moment.

"I'm sorry," Kate told her. "I didn't want to upset you. I just thought it was so beautiful and I'd never seen it before until now and all of a sudden it might just go away again."

She looked at her grandmother. It was hard now to tell from her expression just exactly what was going through her mind. Kate decided it was time to change the subject. "I went to a bonfire last night," she said. "It was really good." She carried on describing the way the red fire had danced against the black sky, the marshmallows floating on the top of the cocoa and toasted in the embers, and how she had met so many people. She described it well because she could see it all clearly in her mind as she spoke, but when Kate turned to look at her grandmother she did not seem to be listening. Her eyes were fixed firmly in front of her.

"Are you tired?" Kate said. She looked at her watch. It was five minutes before eleven o'clock. "I'd better go now, anyway," she said.

Her grandmother's eyes flicked in her direction. She fixed her gaze on Kate. Her face began working, slowly. She was struggling to speak, Kate realised. Nora began to shake with the effort of speaking and her mouth struggled to move. Kate became frightened. Her grandmother was shaking so much, she looked as if the effort might be too much for her. "D ... d ... d ..." she said.

Kate leaned forward, terrified now of what was happening.

"Don't sell," the words were barely audible, but Kate was sure it was what her grandmother had said. Nora slumped back on the bed.

"Don't sell?" Kate said. "That was what you just said, wasn't it?"

Ever so faintly, her grandmother nodded.

"I'll tell Anne what you said," Kate told her, standing up.

Her grandmother made a noise that was somewhere between a moan and a grunt.

Kate looked at her. She had a strong sense that what she had said wasn't enough. Her grandmother didn't want to leave it at that.

"I will tell her," Kate assured her grandmother. Nora's eyes looked back at her beseechingly.

"That isn't enough, is it?" Kate said. "All right, I won't let her sell. Is that OK?"

Her grandmother nodded. She relaxed.

"Goodbye then," Kate said. She turned and walked out of the room. How exactly she was going to change Anne's mind, Kate didn't know. She had been tempted to say to her grandmother that she didn't know how difficult the task was, because she didn't know what Anne was like. But then it occurred to her that of course she did.

Anne was sitting in the car. "How was she?" she asked Kate as soon as she got in.

"She spoke again," Kate told her.

"Did she? What did she say?"

"She said, 'Don't sell'."

Anne stared at her. "What?" she demanded.

"She said, 'Don't sell'," Kate repeated. "She meant the land."

"How could she possibly ..." Anne began. Then she stopped abruptly. "Kate, you didn't tell her something, did you?" she said sharply.

Kate knew immediately that Anne wasn't going to like what she had to say, but she had no alternative now. "I told her that there was a danger the land might have to be sold if she didn't recover properly," Kate began. "I only ..."

Anne interrupted her. "You did *what*?" she demanded. "Kate, are you out of your mind? What the hell did you do that for?"

"I had to," Kate said.

"You had to?" Anne stared at her as if she was from another planet. "I don't believe I'm hearing this," she said. "Kate do you realise that you could have killed her."

"I'm sorry," Kate said, "But ..."

Again Anne's voice cut through her explanation.

"Is she all right?"

144

"Yes. I think so."

"You think so?"

"She is all right," Kate said.

"The shock of hearing a piece of news like that to someone who is just recovering from a stroke!" Anne went on. "I really thought you had more sense than that. I thought I could trust you, Kate."

It was this last remark that really stung Kate. "You never trust me with anything," she said.

Anne looked at her in utter bewilderment. "Kate, what are you talking about? I never trust you with anything. That's absolutely ridiculous, I am always trusting you with situations."

Kate opened her mouth to speak. She wanted to say you won't even trust me enough to tell me about my own father, but she didn't have time. Anne was unstoppable.

"But anyway," she went on, "this is neither the time nor the place to discuss my relationship with you. What we are talking about is my mother, an elderly woman who has just had a stroke and now you get her all worked up over something you have only half understood."

"Maybe I have only half understood it," Kate said, interrupting Anne now, "but if so then that's because I'm only ever told half the truth."

"Look, Kate, I'm not going to go on with this argument. It's completely pointless talking to you while you're in this mood," Anne said. She got out of the car.

"Where are you going?" Kate said.

"I'm going to the hospital to see what sort of a state she's in," Anne told her.

"I'll come with you," Kate said, starting to get up.

"You will not," Anne said, firmly. "I just want you to wait here, please."

She strode away leaving Kate staring after her.

Kate sat back down again and sighed. There was nothing else she could do except wait. Time passed slowly as she sat there in the car park. A few cars came and went, but mostly nothing happened. She just stared out of the windscreen feeling frustrated and unhappy. Every now and again she glanced into the rear-view mirror to see if there was any sign of Anne returning. After about ten minutes she saw her, walking as purposefully back towards the car as she had walked away from it. "She's so determined that she is right about everything," Kate said to herself.

"Well?" Kate said.

"She was asleep," Anne said.

"I told you she was all right," Kate insisted.

"We don't know whether she is or not," Anne said. "For the time being, she's asleep."

"I'm sure she's all right," Kate said. "I don't think it hurts people to tell them the truth."

"Oh, don't you?" Anne said, angrily.

"Please can you not be so angry about it," Kate said, determined to remain calm.

"I am shocked, Kate, not angry," Anne said. She steered the car out of the gates of the car park and on to the road. "Now if you don't mind," she said, "I'd rather not have this conversation and drive at the same time."

Chapter Fourteen

"I THINK YOU'D better not come to the hospital today," Anne announced the next morning as they sat over a breakfast of tea and toast.

"I want to," Kate said.

"The question is what's best for Grandma," Anne said.

"She's my grandmother," Kate said.

"Of course she is," Anne said, as if it was something hardly worth pointing out.

"Then I've got a right to see her," Kate said.

"A right to?" Anne looked at Kate in surprise. "Well I suppose you could say that," she said, "but you're not to upset her."

"I won't," Kate said.

When they arrived in the hospital, Nora was propped up higher in the bed than before. She had been staring unseeingly in front of her as they came through the door, but the moment she caught sight of them, her face became animated. She began the painfully slow process of forming words but this time she did not shake quite so much as her mouth formed the word, "Hello."

"Hello, Mum," Anne said.

Nora nodded. Then her head slowly turned to face Kate. Again she struggled to speak and another word came out. "Kate."

Kate smiled. "Hello," she said.

"Well, you're making great progress," Anne told her, sitting down beside the bed.

There was silence in the room then. It was as if the things that Anne was deliberately not saying prevented all further conversation. Kate cleared her throat nervously. Then Anne spoke. "The weather's very good," she said, with forced cheeriness. "I told Kate to expect rain before we came, but we've hardly seen a drop." There was no response from Nora and again they lapsed into silence.

"It's very hot in London, apparently," Anne said a few moments later. "The tar on the roads has been melting in some places. It was on the news last night."

Her words sounded so feeble and trite and as soon as she had finished speaking the silence swamped them all again. You could hear the ticking of the clock on the wall. Kate found herself watching its second hand jerkily measuring through the divisions of a minute. She looked away from the clock and back at her grandmother. Nora's face took on that intense look of concentration that preceded an attempt to speak. She fixed her eyes on Anne and the words came out painfully slowly. "Is it ...?"

"Is it what?" Anne asked her.

"Is it ...?" Nora seemed to be struggling to remember the right word.

"Do you want to know what day of the week it is?" Anne asked. "Is that it? It's Friday." But this was clearly not what Nora wanted to know.

"Is it ...?" she began again. Her face showed intense frustration as she search for what it was she wanted to say.

"Don't worry about it," Anne suggested, but her mother would not be put off. Her eyes filled up with tears as she strained to communicate. Suddenly she knew what she wanted to say. "Is it Dennis?" she asked.

"Dennis?" Anne said, astonished. She had not expected this. Her mother nodded. "Dennis Carthy, you mean?" she asked. Again Nora nodded. Anne turned to Kate. "This is your fault," she said. She turned back to her mother. "Don't worry about all of that," she said. "You just get yourself better."

But Nora would not be put off. "Is it?" she said again. Her eyes, which were fixed on Anne, had a steely glint in them.

"All right then," Anne said reluctantly. "Dennis Carthy came to see me. He wants to buy the farm. I didn't say yes," she added, seeing the fierce look that came over her mother's face.

Nora struggled to push herself further up the bed. She only seemed able to use one arm properly, but she did not let that deter her. Finally, when she was satisfied with her position, she spoke again. This time it was just one word: "Don't."

"I told you," Anne repeated, "I didn't say yes. Now I don't think this is the time to be having a discussion like this. I think you need to concentrate on getting better."

Nora's eyes were still fixed on Anne in a stare of incredible intensity. She seemed to be trying to burn her thoughts into her daughter's mind. "I won't do anything," Anne told her, "I promise. Not until we're able to talk about it properly." Nora relaxed. "Now then," Anne said, "let's talk about something else, shall we?"

It was hard work making conversation after that, but Anne persisted. She talked about her mother's car, what good condition it was in, how economical on petrol it was, much more economical than her own, and how good it was on bends. She talked about the house, how she had been looking after it, how Kate had found a spider in the bath on her first day, and how a pair of robins kept hopping around near the kitchen window looking for crumbs. "I expect you've been feeding them, haven't you?" she said. Her mother nodded. She looked tired, drained by the effort of communication, and after a while Anne decided it was time for them to leave.

"You see," Kate said, as soon as they got out of the room.

"I see that you've given her something to worry about," Anne told her.

"Don't you think she ought to know?" Kate said.

"Of course she ought to know. It's just a question of the right time."

"I don't think it's done her any harm," Kate insisted.

"If it hasn't, then it's more by luck than good judgement."

The way Anne spoke was as if she were closing a door on the subject. It was always the same with her. She dictated the terms of any discussion. It was so infuriating. She had this thing about being strong, making decisions and sticking to them. The trouble was, the decisions were always hers, even when they concerned Kate. Kate was informed, but never consulted.

Ever since she had seen the poster for the traditional music concert that was to be held this evening, Kate had been wanting to discuss it with Anne. She had tried to broach the subject on a number of occasions, but now she made up her mind to keep the whole thing to herself. After all, Anne kept plenty of things to *her*self.

152

"Liam's calling for me tonight," she said, after they had got into the car.

"Is he?" Anne said, raising her eyebrows. "You didn't waste any time there, did you?" she added playfully.

"Oh, Mum!" Kate complained.

"Only a joke, Kate," Anne said. "Where are you supposed to be going then?"

"To Cruachan. There's a concert on. It's part of the festival I told you about."

"Is it now? And how are you getting in to the town?"

Kate hadn't thought about this.

"I suppose you'll want me to give the pair of you a lift," Anne went on.

"Oh, I don't suppose so," Kate said airily. "I expect Liam will have made some arrangements." She had no idea whether this was true or not but she just felt like asserting her independence.

In fact she was right. Liam had made arrangements. He knocked at the door that evening, and looked very nervous when Anne opened it. "You must be Liam," she said.

He nodded.

"Come on in."

Liam stood in the hall with his hands in his pockets.

"I remember when you were born," she told him. "Not long before I went to England." This piece of

153

information did not make him feel any easier.

"Well, Kate's all ready," Anne said. "Do you want me to give you two a lift to Cruachan?"

"My brother Michael's outside in his van," Liam said. "Thanks very much anyway."

Anne looked slightly disappointed. She always wanted to be in control of everything, Kate thought to herself. "Right, well, look after yourselves," she said.

"I shouldn't think we'll come to much harm in Cruachan," Kate observed.

"No, I suppose not," Anne agreed. "I'll come and pick you up afterwards," she said.

"You needn't bother," Kate replied.

"It's no bother," Anne said firmly.

Kate sighed.

"Let's go then," she told Liam. He turned and opened the door.

"Bye now," Anne said.

"Bye, Mum."

Michael's van smelled a bit of sheep, and it wasn't particularly comfortable. She and Liam had to sit crammed together at the front. But it was better than going in with Anne and being so very close to Liam was quite nice, though a little bit embarrassing.

In the back of the van were what looked like microphone stands as well as coils of heavy black wire and black and silver metal boxes.

154

"You're very versatile, you two," Kate said. "Sheep by day and sound systems by night."

"You have to be versatile," Michael said. Liam said nothing. He still looked as if he was recovering from the experience of knocking for her.

"It's mostly set up already," Michael went on. "We were down there early this afternoon. There's just a little bit of tidying up to do."

"I didn't think they needed amplifiers and stuff for traditional music," Kate said.

"It's a big hall," he explained, "and it will probably be full. Bodies soak up sound."

They drove the rest of the way in silence. Kate stared out into the darkness. Once the headlights caught the eyes of a creature that ran across the road in front of them. Michael braked a little abruptly.

"What was it?" she asked.

"Fox, I think." Michael said.

Kate wondered if it was the same fox that she had heard howling the other night.

The hall was empty when they arrived. A low staging area had been set up at one end and tables and chairs were arranged informally. To the side of the staging area was what Kate assumed must be a mixing deck. Michael and Liam finished setting up the equipment. It took about half an hour. Kate sat on a chair at the back while Liam and Michael set up the stands they had brought, taped down leads which might have tripped people up and checked that everything was working. When they were finished, Michael said, "Shall we go for a drink?"

"Do you fancy that?" Liam asked Kate.

"OK," Kate said.

The three of them went together to the bar in which she and Anne had first met Siobhan's aunt. It was different in the evening, full of people, a hubbub of conversation, laughter. They went to the bar.

"What will you have?" Michael asked. "A double whiskey?" It was a joke and Michael only meant to be nice, but there was something about it that suggested he thought of her as a child. She had not intended to ask for alcohol. She strongly suspected that everyone in the pub would know exactly how old she was.

She had drunk alcohol before, secretly. Her friend Laura's father had so much in the house that he didn't notice when they sampled it. One evening Laura, Emma and herself had tried sherry, gin and rum. Kate had barely tasted them, mainly because she didn't like the taste, but Emma had drunk quite a lot. Then she had got giggly and stupid. Laura and Kate had been forced to take her out of the house into the fresh air. She was sick in the local park. Kate had made up her mind at the time never to be so stupid.

"Have they got any fizzy water?" she asked.

"They have, of course," Michael agreed.

"I'll have that then."

"Right you are."

Michael looked at Liam. "I'll have the same as Kate," he said.

The barman came over, "Three mineral waters," Michael ordered.

"Is that what you normally drink?" Kate asked.

"When we're working," Liam said.

"You'll not get very drunk on that," the barman said.

"We will not," Michael agreed.

"Still," the barman added, expertly picking up three bottles with one hand, and unscrewing the lids with the other. "I expect you're merry enough by yourselves." He poured the water into three tall glasses and added ice and lemon. Michael picked up one and handed it to Kate.

"Thank you," she said.

"You're welcome," he told her.

They went and sat down around a table by themselves.

"This will be the best event of the festival," Liam told her.

"Will it?"

"Yeah. There'll be a disco, a couple maybe, but it's just, you know, chart music."

"I like a lot of chart music," Kate said.

"So do I, but this is impressive. I mean, you should see the guy who's playing. He's been here before, loads

157

of times. He comes from round here. He can play any-thing. Sometimes he just improvises. He's got real …" He searched for the right word.

Kate looked at him expectantly. This could well be her father that Liam was talking about so enthusiastically. Noticing her intense concentration on his words, Liam began to falter. "I mean he's just very good," he finished lamely.

"How's your grandmother?" Michael asked.

"She's making quite a good recovery," Kate told him.

"I'm glad to hear it," he said. "She's a very popular woman, you know."

"Really?" Kate asked.

"Oh yeah. She's got a lot of spirit," he went on. "Running that place on her own."

"Yes, but what will happen to it now?" Kate asked. She didn't suppose that Anne would be very pleased to hear her speculating out loud like this, but she didn't care. Anne wasn't here.

"That's the question," Michael said.

"I can't see how she's going to recover quickly enough to run it," Kate said.

Michael shook his head. "It's a problem, and that's the truth," he said. Quite suddenly he drained his glass and stood up. "I've just remembered something I didn't finish," he said. "I'll see you two later."

Kate guessed that he was inventing this excuse so

that he could leave them together. It was nice of him, she thought.

Although Liam was shy and quiet when other people were around – even Michael – he seemed to relax when he was on his own with Kate. It didn't matter if there was a lull in the conversation from time to time. They just sat back and waited until it started again. Kate was surprised at how much they agreed about things, even though their lives were so different. Liam lived in the middle of the country, in a place where so few people came and went that you knew who each one was and you spoke to them. Kate lived in the middle of the city where you didn't necessarily know the name of your own neighbour, where people lived in apartments in the same house and didn't even speak to each other, except perhaps to exchange the briefest of nods. And yet they felt the same way about so many things. They just seemed to be in harmony with each other. Liam asked her about her friends and Kate found herself telling him about Laura, Emma and Lucy.

"Which is your best friend?" Liam asked.

Kate shook her head. "None of them," she said. "I try to be independent."

Liam thought about this. "That's impressive," he said.

It sounded impressive, Kate thought, but really it was another word for loneliness. But she didn't say that. She didn't want Liam to think of her as a sad little girl who needed friends. "What about you?" she asked him instead.

"I haven't really got a best friend," Liam admitted. "I'm pretty close to Michael, but, you know, that's not the same thing."

"What about Sean?" Kate asked.

"I like Sean," Liam said, "but we're not quite on the same wavelength, not all the time, anyway. Do you know what I mean?"

Kate knew exactly what he meant and she was glad. Sean was not quite on her wavelength either. "Siobhan likes him," she said.

"I know," Liam said. "A bit too keen, I think."

"Why do you say that?" Kate asked.

"It puts him off," Liam said.

"Does it?"

"Of course. Independence is much more attractive."

Kate realised, perhaps a little bit slowly, that this was a compliment. She felt herself blushing. "It's her personality," she said. "She can't help saying whatever's on the top of her head."

"I know," Liam said. "It's the nice thing about her."

They talked about everything and nothing until Liam looked at his watch and suddenly announced that the concert would be starting shortly. Kate had wanted to get there early, wanted to be sure of a place at the front so that she could see the violin player properly.

"Let's go," she said, standing up.

They left the bar and went over to the community centre. Kate was dismayed to see that there was now a queue of people outside, but Liam led her past them.

The hall was already quite full of people but Liam walked through the middle of them. Kate felt very self-conscious, but she followed him. He led her over to the staging area where Michael was already standing with a pair of headphones on.

"What are you going to do?" Kate asked.

"Nothing really," Liam said. "I'm just here in case."

"In case what?"

He shrugged. "In case Michael falls asleep, I suppose," he said. "Let's sit down."

There were a couple of chairs behind the mixing deck and they sat down on these. Kate realised that she would have a perfect view of the musicians when they came on stage.

After a while people stopped coming in at the back of the hall and all the seats were taken. Then the lights in the hall were dimmed, except for those on the staging area. The buzz of conversation which had been filling the place suddenly dropped as a group of musicians walked on to the stage carrying their instruments. There was a guitar player, a man who carried what looked like a flat drum which Kate learned later was called a bodhran, another man carrying something that

161

looked a bit like a set of bagpipes, only smaller, and then the violinist. They stood in front of their microphones, adjusting their instruments to their satisfaction. The violin player was in the centre, a little in front of the others. He was clearly the star of the show.

Kate had not known what to expect and now that she could actually see him things were no clearer. She did not feel any sudden surge of recognition. She did not look at his face and think, "Yes, I look like him!" Instead, she saw a middle-aged man, not bad-looking, but nothing special. He was just dressed in ordinary clothes. He didn't look like a pop star or anything like that. He had dark curly hair and he needed a shave. He smiled at the audience and she could see the lines on his face, but it was a friendly face.

Once the concert had begun, Kate had to admit that Liam had been right: Joe Hendry was very good. The music was sometimes sad and occasionally solemn but mostly it was fast and furious, full of the wildness of the countryside around them, leaping from note to note like a living creature. She closed her eyes and let its passion and energy fill her mind.

The audience applauded loudly at the end of every number, and as the evening wore on, they got more and more enthusiastic. To one side of the hall, Kate saw two little girls, about seven or eight years old, dancing. They were holding their bodies straight with their arms at their sides, but their feet picked out the complicated steps of Irish traditional dancing. They weren't dancing for anyone in particular and no one except Kate was even looking at them. They were just dancing for the joy of it.

Tune followed tune without a break until Kate wondered how the musicians could keep going for so long. But at last the music came to an end and the musicians turned to walk off the stage. Kate felt a surge of panic. She hadn't thought about what she would do when this happened, but she knew that she wanted to do something. They must have gone to a dressing room, she realised. She felt that she had to get up, follow them, knock on the dressing-room door and ask to speak to Joe Hendry, but she couldn't move. She was frozen to her chair. The crowd carried on clapping, cheering and stamping and finally, to Kate's relief, the musicians came back on to the stage to play an encore.

Joe counted them in, "One, two, three, four ..." and they were off again on their last and wildest tune. The spotlight picked out Joe as his bow sawed frantically back and forth and the melody raced away. The audience began to clap in time, and as they did so the music got faster. Everyone was on their feet now as a current of excitement swept through the hall. And then, suddenly, they stopped. There was a moment's silence and then a great cheer went up from the audience and once again the musicians walked off the stage. This time, Kate felt certain, the concert was really over. They would not be coming back for another encore. This was it.

She stood up. "I'll see you later," she told Liam. She turned and walked off in the direction that the musicians had taken. They had gone through a door at the back of the hall and Kate followed. She found herself in a corridor with a number of doors opening off it. Kate stopped. From behind one of the doors she could hear someone talking and someone else laughing. She walked over to the door, took a deep breath and knocked.

The laughter stopped. Then the door opened and a face peered around it. It was not Joe but one of the other musicians, the one who played the pipes. "Can I speak to Joe?" she asked.

He turned back to the people in the room. "There's a girl here for you, Joe," he called out.

The pipe player went away and Joe Hendry himself came out. He stood in the doorway, looking at her.

"Hello," she said. "I'm Kate."

She had hoped that might be enough; that he might smile and say, "Not that Kate, surely?" But he just smiled and said "Hello, Kate," and then, since she stood there unable to say anything else, he said, "Did you want an autograph?"

Kate shook her head.

"Well what can I do for you?"

"I think you used to be a friend of my mother's,"

Kate said. She knew that she sounded peculiar.

"A friend of your mother's? Is that so?"

"Her name is Anne Gallagher."

"Anne Gallagher?" The expression on his face changed. The indulgent look meant for an enthusiastic fan disappeared and his face became serious. "Let's go somewhere and talk," he said.

He led the way down the corridor. He tried the handle of the next door along, but it was locked. They went on a bit further until he found a door that opened. "After you," he said, holding the door wide.

Kate went inside. It was a small room that looked as if it was used for meetings. There wasn't much inside except a table, some chairs and a notice board. They stood inside looking at each other, then Joe said, "Let's sit down, shall we?"

They sat down on either side of the table and looked at each other with curiosity. Then Joe said, "Is Anne home then?"

"Yes."

"That's nice."

"Her mother's ill."

"I'm sorry. Is she in a bad way?"

"She's had a stroke."

"That's a pity. I was fond of her. Is this your first time in Ireland?"

"Yes."

The conversation didn't seem to be going in the

direction she wanted.

Joe looked thoughtful. "I'd like to see your mother again," he said.

Kate felt a flash of anger. "What about me?" she said.

"Sorry?" Joe looked confused.

"What about me?" Kate repeated. "Aren't you pleased to see me?"

"Very pleased," Joe said, but he said it as if he thought she was behaving a little oddly.

"Why didn't you ever get in touch before?" Kate demanded.

"With your mother?" Joe said.

"Yes," Kate said, "with my mother." Then she changed her mind. She decided to confront him. "No," she said, "with me. Why didn't you ever get in touch with me?"

Joe still looked confused. "I never knew you existed," he said. "But I'm very pleased to meet you now."

His politeness only made Kate angry. "Pleased to meet me!" she exclaimed. "Is that all you can say?"

Joe frowned. "What do you mean?" he asked. "What else can I say?"

Kate shrugged. "I don't know," she said. "I just thought ... well, you meet your own daughter for the first time and you say that you're pleased to—"

"Just a minute," Joe interrupted. "What did you say?"

"I said you meet your own daughter for the first time and all you can say is that—"

Joe interrupted her again. "Daughter!" he said. "Are you saying that you're my daughter?"

Suddenly all the conviction drained out of Kate. She felt as if a wave of cold water had just washed over her. Perhaps she had got it all wrong. "I ... I thought you were," she said hesitantly. "I'm sorry, maybe I just ... Oh, God! I think I'd better go." She stood up abruptly.

"Wait!" Joe said. He looked at her with an expression that she couldn't fathom. "Sit down, please."

Kate sat back down again.

"Can I just get this straight?" Joe said. "Anne told you that I was your father?"

Kate shook her head. "Not exactly. She said my father was a musician and his name was Joe Hendry."

"That's me," Joe said. "There isn't another Joe Hendry." He shook his head slowly. "Why?" he said, softly. "Why?"

"Why what?"

"Why didn't she tell me?"

"You mean you really didn't know?" Now it was Kate's turn to be surprised.

"Of course I didn't know. Do you think I wouldn't have wanted to see my own daughter?"

"I don't know," Kate said. She had a lump in her throat and it was a struggle to get the words out.

"One day she just told me it was all over between

us," he said. His eyes were looking into the distance as if he could see the scene being played out all over again. "She said she was going to England. There was nothing I could say to talk her out of it. She'd made up her mind."

It sounded just like Anne.

"That was all I knew. I swear." He looked her straight in the eyes. "Do you believe me, Kate?"

Kate nodded.

"I'm sorry, Kate. Really I am."

Kate opened her mouth to speak but as she did so the door opened. Anne stood there in the doorway looking at them both. Her face was flushed and she looked angry.

Chapter Fifteen

AT FIRST all three of them were silent. Then Joe spoke. "Hello, Anne," he said.

"Hello, Joe." She turned to Kate. "I've been looking for you," she said. "Nobody seemed to know where you'd gone." Her voice was hard and brittle.

"I didn't tell anyone," Kate said.

"So what's going on?" she demanded.

"I wanted to see Joe," Kate said.

"Why didn't you tell me?"

"Hold on there, just a minute," Joe said. "Why didn't she tell you? I think that's a bit rich coming from you, isn't it?"

"You stay out of this, Joe," Anne said sharply. "It's got nothing to do with you."

Joe stood up to face her. "It's got everything to do with me," he said, "from what I hear."

Anne turned to Kate. Her eyes flashed with controlled anger. "What have you been telling him?" she asked.

At first Kate had been taken aback by Anne's entrance. Now she made up her mind not to let her mother intimidate her. "Just what you told me," she said, "that my father was a musician and his name was Joe Hendry."

"It's a pity you didn't tell me that, Anne, isn't it?" Joe demanded.

Kate looked from Anne to Joe.

"No, it isn't a pity," Anne told him. "I knew what I was doing."

"Is that right?" Joe said bitterly.

"Yes it is."

They stood face to face, glaring at each other. "Oh, Joe," Anne said, softening a very little bit. "We were too young."

"No we weren't," Joe insisted.

"We weren't committed to each other."

"You didn't give us a chance to find out."

Anne sighed. "Because there was no point," she insisted. "I didn't want to go tagging all round the country after you. You wouldn't have wanted me to."

"I didn't get a choice, though, did I?" Joe said.

"What about me?" Kate demanded suddenly. She had been listening to them both and neither of them seemed to be giving the slightest consideration to her feelings. They both turned and looked at her.

"I was doing what was best for you," Anne told her. She reached out her hand to put it on Kate's shoulder. Angrily, Kate shrugged it off.

"No you weren't," she said. "You were doing what suited you, like you always do."

Anne was stung by this. "Thank you very much," she said.

"It's true," Kate said. "You don't ask anyone else what they want. You just tell people." Anne looked back at her, without speaking. Kate could see that what she had to say was hitting home. "I had a right to meet my father."

"I would have—" Anne began.

"No you wouldn't," Kate said. "You would have just kept putting it off. It was only because of Grandma's stroke that we're here at all."

"You didn't want to come, remember," Anne said, seizing on this as if it were important.

"I didn't know anything about it, did I?" Kate said.

Anne could find no answer to this. She stood there for a moment, then she took a deep breath and slowly nodded her head. "All right," she said. She was looking at the ground and she spoke as if it were a real effort to force the words out. "Maybe you're right." Now she looked up and faced Kate. "I'm sorry," she said.

"Listen," Joe said, "this place is closing soon. Can we go somewhere and talk – properly, I mean?"

"Let's go home," Kate said.

Anne looked a little surprised. "Back to the farm, you mean?" she said.

"Yes."

"I suppose we could."

"Right. I'll just go and tell the others what's happening," Joe said. "I won't be a minute." He walked over to the door, then turned to look at them. "Don't go away, will you?" he said.

"Don't be ridiculous, Joe," Anne replied.

"I wouldn't put it past you," Joe said.

"We won't go," Kate said determinedly. Anne gave her a look but said nothing. Joe disappeared.

There was silence in the room after he had gone. Neither Anne nor Kate seemed to know what to say next. Then he came back. "OK," he said. "I'm ready."

When they got to the car, Anne said, "You'd better sit in the back, Joe. Kate and I will sit in the front."

"I'll sit in the back with Joe," Kate said, opening the car door and getting in. She had made up her mind: from now on she was going to do what she wanted.

Anne looked put out, but she said nothing. She got into the driver's seat and Joe got in beside Kate.

For a long time there was silence in the car, except for the sound of the engine. Then Joe spoke. "Do you like Ireland?" he asked.

"Everyone asks me that all the time," Kate said.

"I suppose they do," Joe said. "It's hard to know how else to start a conversation," he said.

"I thought your playing was really brilliant," Kate told him. It was the truth. Throughout the concert she had been thinking about this meeting, anxious about what it would be like, nevertheless she could not help noticing how good he was.

"Thank you very much," Joe said.

"And doesn't he know it?" Anne said from the front of the car. It was said as a joke, but with a hard edge.

"I'm passionate about my music," Joe said defensively. "That's all."

"That's a good thing," Anne said, "if you only have yourself to think about."

"What's that supposed to mean?" Joe asked.

"You know what I mean, Joe. Music was everything to you. You never wanted anything else."

"You never asked me what I wanted," Joe said.

"Back to that again," Anne said with an exasperated tone.

"Of course we're back to that," Joe said, "because it's the simple truth."

"Can we stop this, please?" Kate said.

"You were the one who started it," Anne said.

"And I was right to," Kate said. "You've just said sorry."

"All right, but I still wish you'd spoken to me about it first."

"Mum, don't be ridiculous!" Kate said, starting to get angry herself. "You wouldn't have let me."

"You don't know that."

"Shall we talk about it properly when we get back?" Joe said.

They both agreed and nothing more was said on the way home.

They finally got back to the farm and parked the car in the garage. They were standing on the doorstep waiting for Anne to open the front door when she hesitated and then turned to Joe. "I want to say one thing to Kate on her own," she said. "Could you just wait outside for a moment?"

"Please yourself," Joe said. "Just don't make it too long," he said. "It's cold out here."

Anne opened the door and gestured for Kate to go inside.

"What do you want to say to me?" Kate asked stubbornly.

"I'll tell you inside." She stood there waiting for Kate to go in first.

Anne was still insisting on doing things her way. Kate shrugged and went inside, but she looked annoyed as she did so.

In the kitchen Anne said, "I just want to make one thing perfectly clear, Kate. If you've got hold of any crazy idea about bringing your parents together, then I want you to forget it, right now."

"I haven't got any idea like that," Kate said.

"Oh." Anne sounded a little deflated. Then she added. "Good, because there's no point."

Kate said nothing. She wasn't going to get dragged into the argument between Anne and Joe.

"Right then, I'll let Joe in."

Joe came in and stood in the middle of the kitchen looking around him. Then he said, "I was standing outside, thinking. You and Kate and myself all disagree, right?"

"Who says that Kate and I disagree?" Anne demanded.

"I do," Kate said.

"Well then," Joe continued, "why don't we just agree to differ for now, and talk about something else."

Anne still looked unhappy.

"We're only going round and round in circles," Joe insisted.

"That depends on how you look at it," Anne said.

"That's my point, exactly," Joe said. "We both look at it differently. So let's just change the subject."

Anne shrugged.

"Is that OK with you, Kate?" Joe went on. "Just for the time being, at any rate?"

"I think it's a good idea," Kate said.

"Right then," Joe went on, "what shall we talk about?"

There was silence. No one could think of anything to say that didn't sound silly or somehow wrong. The silence grew longer and longer. It seemed to hang in the air between them, filling the room. Then Kate suddenly

175

realised there was something else she wanted to talk about. "What's going to happen to the farm?" she said.

"That depends," Anne said evasively.

"Is it because of your mother being ill?" Joe asked.

"Yes, but I'll sort it out," Anne said.

"I want to know what's going to happen," Kate said.

"I'd rather discuss it another time," Anne said.

"Well I wouldn't."

Anne took one of her deep breaths. "It hasn't got anything to do with Joe, has it?" she asked.

"That's true," Joe said, "but, you know, I might be able to help."

"You?" Anne said. "How could you help?"

Joe opened his hands in a shrug. "Tell me the problem," he said. "It can't hurt, can it?"

"All right," Anne agreed reluctantly. "My mother's not going to be able to look after this place any longer," she went on.

"She might," Kate said. "When she gets better."

"Kate," Anne said. "I don't think she's ever going to get that much better. The farm was hopelessly run down as it was. It was only the fact that the neighbours helped out that it kept going at all."

Kate said nothing. It sounded so true.

"A man called Dennis Carthy is prepared to buy the place," Anne said. "He advised me to get power of attorney and sell it to him."

"Is that what you want to do then?" Joe asked.

"No!" Kate said.

"Kate, be sensible," Anne said.

"I don't want you to sell the farm," Kate said. "I've just discovered it and now you want to get rid of it again."

"I don't want to, Kate," Anne insisted. "It's not a matter of wanting. But what else can I do?"

"When I go back to England," Kate said. "I'll want to come back to Ireland and if the farm is sold, where will I go?"

"You can come and stay with me any time you like," Joe said.

That stopped Anne in her tracks. She didn't like the idea of Kate staying with Joe one little bit. "All right then, what else do you suggest?" she said after a moment.

Joe laughed bitterly. "You wouldn't want to encourage her to see too much of me, now would you?"

"It isn't that," Anne said. "Maybe Kate has a point, that's all." She turned to Kate. "The thing is," she said, "do you have an alternative suggestion?"

Kate was silent. Anne always seemed able to out-argue her. It was so infuriating. Then Joe spoke again. "You say that the neighbours are good?" he said.

"They're great," Anne said.

"Do I know them?" he asked.

"I'm sure you do. Aidan and Margaret."

177

Joe thought hard. "I remember Aidan, sort of," he said. "Is it just themselves?"

"They have two boys."

"They're the ones who did the sound for the concert," Kate said.

"Michael and Liam?" Joe asked.

"That's right."

"Of course I know them," Joe said. "Michael's got sheep, hasn't he?"

"Loads of them," Kate put in.

"Well why don't you see if he wants to rent the land?" Joe suggested.

"Who says he wants to rent any land?" Anne asked him.

"No one," Joe said. "But the more land you have, the more sheep you can graze. Anyone knows that, and he looks like the kind of fellow who enjoys hard work." He grinned. "Unlike myself."

Anne smiled and it was a genuine smile. "That's the truth," she told him. "You were never much good with a spade or a shovel, Joe Hendry."

"I'm a fiddler," he told her. He turned to Kate. "Did you ever hear the poem, 'The Fiddler of Dooney'?" he asked her.

Kate shook her head. "No," she said.

" 'When I play on my fiddle in Dooney, folk dance like a wave of the sea'," he intoned. "That's how it begins."

"Listen to him," Anne said. "He was the same when I knew him. Full of blarney and moonshine."

"Poetry and music, that's what they're called," Joe insisted. He winked at Kate. "You're a hard woman, Anne Gallagher," he told her.

"I'm a realist, that's all."

"Have it your own way," Joe said. "Anyhow, would you like me to mention it to Michael?"

"You?"

"Why not? I'd only put it to him fair and square that you might be looking for a tenant."

"I think he should," Kate said to Anne.

Anne thought hard about it. Finally she shrugged. "OK," she said. "What have I got to lose?"

They carried on talking for a long time after that. Joe asked Anne what she was doing in England and she explained about the café.

"I can't imagine you running a café," Joe had said.

"She does a really good job," Kate said. For some reason she had felt obliged to say this. Perhaps it was out of a sense of fair play. Anne looked pleased, even though she tried not to let it show.

"I'm sure she does," Joe agreed.

He asked a few more questions about the café and Anne described it in more detail. "You know what you could do with, don't you?" Joe said with a smile.

"No, but I'm pretty sure you're about to tell me," Anne said.

"Live music," Joe went on.

"I should have guessed," Anne said. She sounded both exasperated and amused.

"It would bring in the customers," Joe said.

"I've got enough customers already, thank you," Anne said.

"Just a suggestion," Joe said.

"Do you still live around here?" Kate asked him.

Joe shook his head. "I've got a flat in Dublin. It's not very big, but it's nice. You'd like Dublin," he told her.

"Would I?"

"You'd love it," he went on. "But actually I'm not there that much. I do a lot of touring."

"Where do you play?"

He made a sweeping gesture with his hands. "All over Europe, especially Holland. They love me in Holland."

"Is that right?" Anne said, raising one eyebrow in a gesture that Kate had never seen her use before. It made her look slightly teasing. If Anne was not too old for that sort of thing, Kate would almost have described it as a 'flirty' look.

"They do. I sell more records there than any-where."

"Do you make records?" Kate asked in surprise.

"I do of course," he said. "Don't get the wrong idea, I'm not a pop star."

"We didn't think you were," Anne said.

Joe looked ever so slightly wounded by her quick dismissal of him. "All the same," he said, "I've come a long way since you knew me, Anne."

"We both have," she told him.

Chapter Sixteen

IT WAS the smell of cooking that woke Kate the next morning and for a moment she thought she was back in London in the flat above The Hideaway. Then she remembered the events of the night before. She got up, dressed and went downstairs. Anne was frying bacon and eggs. Joe was nowhere to be seen.

"Sleep well?" Anne asked.

"Very well," Kate told her. "Where's Joe?"

"He's gone."

"Already?" Kate said.

"Actually, Kate, it's half past eleven," Anne told her.

"Is it? Then why do I feel so tired?"

"Keeping secrets," Anne said. "It makes you tired."

Kate thought about this. It was meant to be a joke, she realised. "You should know," she said.

Anne opened her mouth to speak, then shut it again. She busied herself moving the bacon about in the frying pan. "Fifteen love to me," Kate thought to herself, but she didn't say so aloud. From now on she was going to hold her own with Anne, but there was no point in overdoing it.

"Did he say where he was going?" Kate asked, sitting down at the table.

"He's got to go to another gig this evening in Galway. That's what he's like, here one moment, gone the next."

Kate thought about this for a moment, then she said, "Where did he sleep?"

She had been the first to go to bed the previous night, worn out with the emotional stress of it all.

Anne turned round indignantly. "He slept downstairs," she said angrily.

"I only asked," Kate protested.

"Well just don't start getting any ideas," Anne said.

"Are you going in to the hospital today?" Kate asked, changing the subject.

"Yes."

"I'm coming with you."

When they arrived at the hospital the doctor was just finishing examining Kate's grandmother. They waited in the corridor outside.

"She's doing very well," he told them when he did come out. "We'll be arranging physiotherapy and occupational therapy now."

"What does that mean?" Kate asked.

"Just exercises and things to do to help her recover."

"She definitely will recover then?" Kate asked.

"Well, you can't ever say definitely," the doctor went on, "but she is out of the real danger period now. Generally, if people come through the first few days without another stroke, it's a good sign."

"How long do you think she's likely to be in hospital?" Anne asked.

"It's hard to say," he said. "A few weeks yet, anyhow."

Then he went on his way. Kate and Anne went into the room. Kate's grandmother was propped up on her pillows. She smiled when she saw them, then she said slowly and hesitantly, "Hello, Kate." She looked very pleased with herself, as if she had been practising.

"Hello," Kate said.

Nora turned her head to face Anne. "Hello, Anne," she said.

"Hello, Mum," Anne replied.

They sat down on either side of the bed and then Kate began. "I met my father last night for the first time," she announced.

Her grandmother looked hard at her and Kate could see that she was taking the idea in, thinking about what it meant, remembering.

Anne looked anxious. "Kate," she hissed, "I wish you'd give me some warning before you drop these bombshells."

"I believe in telling people the truth," Kate replied calmly. She turned back to her grandmother. "He's a musician," she went on. "Did you know that?"

Nora opened her mouth and struggled to speak, "Anne wouldn't ..." she began.

"Anne wouldn't tell you?" Kate supplied the words for her. Her grandmother nodded. "I can believe that," Kate said. She looked into her grandmother's eyes. "Were you very angry when you found out – about me, I mean?"

Nora shook her head. She seemed to be searching for the right word. Then she said, "Ashamed."

Kate was stung by this. She felt as if her grandmother had been ashamed of her, of her life. "And are you still ashamed?" she asked.

Her grandmother shook her head. "I was wrong," she said.

Kate looked at the old woman lying in the bed and she suddenly felt that she could forgive her. It was an odd feeling. She looked at Anne and saw tears running down her face. Anne reached forward and took her mother's hand. "I know how hard that is to say," she said. It was a moment of complete understanding. Kate put her own hand on top of her mother's and her grandmother's.

After lunch Siobhan turned up. She gave Kate a very

funny look when she arrived. She came into the house but didn't want to sit down and she seemed ill at ease. Finally she said to Kate, "Would you like to go for a walk?"

She obviously wanted to get out of Anne's earshot, so Kate agreed. She put on her coat and they set off along the route to the turf bog.

"What happened last night?" Siobhan asked when they were outside.

Kate looked at her in surprise. "How do you know about it?" she asked.

"I don't," Siobhan said. "That's why I'm asking. You don't have to tell me if you don't want to, but Liam is a friend of mine." She said this with a very slight toss of her head.

"Oh no! Liam!" Kate said. She had completely forgotten about him. She realised that she had simply got up and walked away without telling him.

"He was really upset," Siobhan said. "I could tell, even though he was trying not to show it."

"Poor Liam," Kate said, dismayed.

"Did you argue with him?" Siobhan asked.

"No," Kate said.

"Was he, you know, hands all over the place?"

Kate laughed. "No, he wasn't," she said.

"I didn't think so," Siobhan said. "He's not the type. Then what happened?" she asked.

Kate hesitated.

"If you don't want to tell me ..." Siobhan began, looking hurt.

"I do," Kate said. "But ..."

"But what?"

"But it's a long story," Kate said.

"I like long stories."

So Kate explained. To her surprise Siobhan did not seem to find the story quite so incredible. "After all," she said, "it was likely to be somebody from round here, wasn't it?"

"I suppose so."

"What do you think of him?" Siobhan asked.

"I like him," Kate said.

"What do you think he'll be like as a father?" Siobhan asked.

"I don't know," Kate said. "I'll just have to wait and see."

"It must be really weird," Siobhan said, "suddenly getting a father at your age."

"It is a bit," Kate agreed.

"I sometimes feel like changing mine," Siobhan went on. "But I suppose he's all right, really. A bit predictable."

"Mine's not predictable," Kate said. "But he might be fun."

"What are you going to tell Liam?" Siobhan asked.

"The truth, of course," Kate replied. "I'm always going to tell people the truth."

Siobhan thought about this. "All the time?" she asked.

"All the time," Kate said.

"Even if it hurts?" Siobhan asked.

Kate nodded her head. "Even if it hurts," she said.

That evening, after Siobhan had left, there was a knock at the front door. It was Michael. He came, he said, because he had heard from Joe that Anne might be prepared to let the land.

"Come in," Anne told him.

When he had come inside, Michael said to Kate. "Liam's outside in the van, if you want to see him."

"I do want to see him," Kate said. She got up and went outside.

Liam was sitting in the van with his eyes closed, so he did not see her approach. She knocked on the window. He jumped and opened his eyes. Kate opened the door and got into the van.

"I want to explain," she said straight away.

"OK," Liam said.

She told him and, amazingly, he understood. "It must have been really important for you," he said.

"It was," she said.

"I thought I must have done something wrong," Liam said. "But I didn't know what it was. I kept going over everything, trying to work it out."

"Poor Liam." She leaned forward and kissed him

on the cheek.

He looked embarrassed and pleased at the same time. "Does that mean …?" he hesitated.

"Does it mean what?"

"I just wondered," he said, "if you'd be interested in …"

Kate laughed. "Going to the disco?" she said.

"Yes."

Kate grinned. She wasn't sure who had asked who, but it didn't matter. "I'd like to very much," she said.

Chapter Seventeen

KATE'S GRANDMOTHER was a determined woman. In the days that followed, Kate began to see just how determined. She watched as Nora fought her way back to the normal world, the world that Kate had always taken for granted in which walking, talking, eating and all the other day-to-day tasks were something you did without thinking.

The first thing that improved was her speech. It was still hesitant and slurred, but there were no more of those terrible struggles for words that had made her whole body shake. She listened when Kate told her what she had been doing and she asked questions about the house, the farm and her neighbours. She smiled when Kate told her about Liam's invitation to the disco.

"He's a nice boy," she said.

On the evening of the disco Kate couldn't decide what to wear. She hadn't brought a lot of clothes with her and nothing that she tried on looked right. She spent ages standing in front of the mirror in a skirt and top that she had always thought suited her but tonight there was something unsatisfactory about it. She went into the kitchen where Anne was sitting reading a newspaper.

"What do you think of this outfit?" she asked.

"Lovely," Anne said.

"Really?"

"Definitely."

Kate went back to her bedroom and looked at herself in the mirror. It wasn't easy because the mirror was only a little one and it mostly showed Kate her head and shoulders. She tried putting her hair up but decided that it looked too much. She shook it out again and sighed. She was beginning to wish she hadn't agreed to go in the first place.

A car horn sounded. She pulled back the curtain and looked out. She could see Michael's van parked outside and Liam looking out of the passenger window. "I'll just have to do as I am," she said to herself. She went downstairs and opened the door.

"You won't be late, will you?" Anne asked.

"No, Mum."

"You are getting a lift back, aren't you?"

"Yes, Mum."

"You're sure you don't want me to come and pick you up?"

"Certain."

"All right then," Anne said reluctantly. "Have a nice time."

Like the concert, the disco was held in the community centre. When they arrived the tables and chairs had been moved away and dance music was pumping out of the speakers. The centre was packed with young people. Kate was surprised at how crowded it was.

"They come from miles around to the festival disco," Liam told her.

Michael went to chat with the DJ about the sound system and they were left to themselves.

"Shall we dance?" Liam asked her.

"Okay."

Liam was a good dancer. That was a relief. She had been a little bit worried in case he turned out to be the sort of boy who stands there like a block of wood, shifting from one foot to the other, completely out of time with the music. He wasn't self-conscious and he wasn't a show-off either. Kate relaxed and let the music take over.

More and more people poured into the centre as they danced. Soon there was hardly room to move. Kate was starting to get hot and tired. "Do you fancy something to drink?" Liam asked her. She could only just hear his voice above the sound of the music but she nodded eagerly.

"What do you want?" he asked.

"Anything," she said. "Just so long as it's cold."

Liam made his way to the bar and stood there waiting to be served. Kate looked around her at the crowd of young people caught up in the music, moving their arms and legs as if they were in a trance. It was such a contrast to the miles of empty countryside that surrounded the little town of Cruachan.

At last Liam came back with the drinks. "Shall we have these outside?" he asked.

"Good idea."

It was deliciously cool outside. Kate stood looking up at the night sky. "I still can't believe how bright the stars are," she said.

But Liam wasn't looking at the stars. He was looking straight at Kate. "I think you're really lovely," he said. Then he looked down at the ground, embarrassed by what he had said.

"Thank you," Kate replied, embarrassed too.

There was silence then between them. Neither of them could think of anything else to say. Other couples walked past, talking and laughing.

They stood there for a little while longer but it was as if everything that there was to say had already been said. At last Kate spoke. "I'm getting cold," she said.

"So am I."

"Shall we go back in?"

"Okay."

They turned to go back and as they did so, Liam

took her hand. This time neither of them was embarrassed. It seemed perfectly natural.

Once they were inside the music made further conversation impossible. They began dancing again but Kate no longer even noticed the music. Her mind was full of what Liam had said. It was the strangest and most wonderful thing that had happened in all of the holiday.

When she lay in bed that night she could not sleep, even though she was quite exhausted. "He thinks I'm lovely," she told herself over and over again and she knew that he meant it. It was something that she would never forget.

It had grown bright outside before she finally did go to sleep and it seemed only a few minutes later that Anne was waking her up.

"You look half dead," Anne told her over breakfast.

"I feel fine." It was true. She felt as if she had had a really good night's sleep.

"You don't have to come to the hospital if you don't want to," Anne said.

"I do want to," Kate insisted.

The physiotherapist was with Nora when they arrived. She told them that they were going to try to get Nora walking.

"Isn't it a bit soon?" Anne asked, but the physiotherapist seemed confident. "It's best to start as soon as possible," she told them. "The longer you leave it, the harder it is. Nora's ready to give it a try, aren't you?"

Nora nodded, but she looked anxious.

"Sit up then," the physiotherapist told her.

Nora sat up. The physiotherapist leaned forward and put one hand under Nora's shoulder. Slowly she helped Nora to her feet. Then she transferred her weight on to a metal walking frame which was standing beside the bed.

"There now," the physiotherapist announced. "Let's just see how long you can stand, shall we?"

It wasn't very long before Nora began to tremble.

"OK, that's grand," the physiotherapist said. She and Kate supported Nora again as she slumped backwards on to the bed. Kate saw that there were tears in her grandmother's eyes.

"I never said it was going to be easy," the physiotherapist said in a kindly voice. "But you'll get there."

Nora nodded her head, slowly and sadly, as if she found it hard to believe what the physiotherapist had told her.

But the next day she was ready to try again. And it wasn't long before she managed to walk a few paces. It took her a full five minutes to travel a distance that Kate could have jumped. She dragged one foot after the other and then stopped, exhausted.

"Well done!" the physiotherapist said. "You'll be walking out of here soon."

She and Kate helped Nora sit back down on the bed, but this time there was a smile on her face. It was still lop-sided. Her smile would always look like that now, the muscles in her face would never work properly again, but what did that matter when she had succeeded in walking? Kate bent over her and kissed her. "Well done, Grandma," she said.

Three weeks later Anne and Kate drove to the hospital in the morning and found Nora dressed and sitting in a wheelchair, waiting for them. She looked up as soon as they came into the ward, her blue eyes glinting like a bird's.

"You look as though you've been ready for hours," Anne said.

It was hard to believe that this was the same woman Kate had seen connected to plastic tubes and monitoring equipment on the evening they had first arrived. In her own clothes she looked, for the first time, not like a patient but like a member of the outside world, the world beyond the hospital gates.

"I've been ready since the doctor made his rounds," she told them.

"Well let's not waste any more time then," Anne said.

Kate took her grandmother's bag and Anne pushed the wheelchair down the ward between the two rows of beds. One by one the other women in the ward sat up in bed and called their goodbyes to Nora. The nurses came out of their office to see her off. "Don't be coming back, now," one of them said with a broad smile.

"I won't," Nora told her.

They took the lift to the ground floor and went out through the automatic glass doors at the front of the building. It was a warm day with just a little wind. Above them in the blue sky a flock of birds wheeled. Anne stopped pushing the wheelchair and they all three looked up as the birds changed direction with perfect timing. Kate looked at her grandmother. Her eyes were still following the flight of the birds, and Kate thought she could see how precious this moment must seem to her. She had so nearly relinquished her hold on life but somehow she had held on. At that moment Nora turned and looked at Kate. She smiled her lop-sided smile. "It's a beautiful day," she said.

Kate nodded. "It certainly is," she replied.

In spite of Anne's disapproval Joe kept coming back. Over the next couple of weeks he returned to the farm frequently. It was never for very long. He was always on his way to or from another gig. Sometimes he looked tired, as if he had driven for hours to get there. Other times he was full of high spirits, telling jokes and teasing Anne for the stern looks she gave him.

A few days after her grandmother had come home, Kate and Anne had just finished breakfast downstairs and Nora had eaten hers on a tray in her bedroom. Kate was sitting at the table feeling sad. It was just beginning to hit her that it was all going to end on the day she went back to England. In the six weeks she had spent at the farm so much had happened. She had gained a grandmother and a father. She had made a whole new set of friends, two of them very special. And very soon it would all be over.

She was thinking of this when there came a knock on the back door. It was Joe. He stood on the doorstep, smiling. He was carrying a violin in one hand and a bow in the other.

"Come in," Kate said.

Joe stepped into the kitchen and held out the violin. "I've brought you a present," he said, offering it to her.

"But I can't play," Kate said. All the same, she was pleased with the present.

"You can learn though," Joe said. "Only if you feel like it, of course," he said. "If not, you could always put it on the wall. It's the one I learned to play on. A bit of family history, you might say." He looked at Anne as he said this, but she made no comment.

"Thank you," Kate said. "Aren't you going to sit down?"

"I can't," he said. "I'm on my way to the airport. I'll tell you what, though, I've been sitting behind a wheel for the last three hours: I wouldn't mind a walk. Do you fancy keeping me company?"

"OK," Kate agreed.

They took the road up towards the turf bog. On the way Joe said, "I might have some gigs lined up in London in the autumn."

"Really?" Kate said.

"It's not certain yet. But if I do, I'll call in and see you when I'm there. If that's all right with you," he added.

When they reached the top they sat side by side with their backs against the lichen-covered stones, the wind rushing up the hill and over them.

"I really love this place," Kate told him.

"Why wouldn't you?" Joe said. "It's your home."

In a field below them they could see Michael's sheep. Three lambs, which had got separated from their mother, ran frantically back towards her, bleating piteously.

"It's not really, though, is it?" Kate said. "I mean, I don't belong here. I wasn't born here."

"You belong where you want to be," Joe told her.

"What about you, Joe?" Kate asked. She had thought about calling him Dad, tried it out even when she was by herself, but it sounded false somehow. So in the end she had settled for Joe.

"What about me?" he asked.

"Where do you belong?"

Joe shrugged. "Wherever people want to hear me play, I suppose," he said.

Kate felt a stab of disappointment. Perhaps Anne was right about him, after all. For all his promises he could never be tied down.

"Do you think that you and Anne will ever ...?" she left the sentence unfinished.

Joe grinned. "Not if Anne has anything to do with it." He took her hands and cupped them in his. "Don't be too disappointed in us," he said.

"I'm not disappointed," she told him. "Really I'm not."

He let go of her again. "Maybe she's right, anyway," he went on. "Anne and I weren't made for each other."

"But it doesn't mean you can't be friends, does it?" Kate said.

"Of course not. We will be great friends, in time."

Kate wasn't sure about that. "Great friends?" she said doubtfully.

"Well maybe just good friends," Joe admitted with a grin. "Anyhow, I know one thing: I won't let the two of you go again, now that I've found you. I'll always be around."

"It was me that found you," Kate reminded him.

"That's true," Joe admitted. "All the same, I promise to keep in touch."

"Even when I'm in England?"

"Even when you're in England. I told you, I'll see you in the autumn."

Kate wondered whether or not she could believe him.

"You've got to give me a chance, Kate," he told her.

She nodded. "OK," she said. "I'll see you in the autumn then."

Joe got up and began walking down the way they had come. "We'd better get back before Anne decides I've kidnapped you," he said.

Kate jumped up and followed him. It would always be like this, she realised. She would be in between the two of them, like a bridge between two different worlds. It was hardly a fairy-tale ending with a perfect family at the end. But maybe it was enough, she reflected. After all, it was the truth, and that was what she had always wanted.

And so, finally, the day came to leave. Aidan arrived to take them to the station in his battered old car. Anne and Kate stood outside the house with their coats on and their luggage all packed. Liam had come too, to say goodbye to Kate.

"We could write to each other," he suggested. "If you like, I mean."

"We could," Kate agreed. "Though I'm not much good at writing letters."

"You can't be worse than me," Liam said. "I can't remember when I last wrote a letter."

Kate smiled. She remembered the letter she had

copied out seven times on the train from Dublin and its promise: 'After some days a boy will ask you out or tell you he loves you.' "It came true," she said out loud.

"What did?" Liam asked.

"Never mind," she told him. "Anyway, if we don't write, I'm coming back."

"Honestly?" Liam said.

"Honestly," she told him. She bent forward and kissed him gently on the lips. The car engine started up.

"Goodbye, Liam," she said. Kate picked up her bag and got into the back of the car beside Anne. She rolled down the window. "See you soon," she told him.

She kept looking out of the window until the car turned round the corner at the bottom of the drive. Then she turned round and sat back down.

"We're going home at last," Anne said.

Kate did not reply. She was thinking about what Joe had said: that you belong where you want to be. She had a feeling that somehow home had shifted for her. It was not just the flat above the café in the middle of London. She would be glad to get back to all that, in a way. She would have something to tell Laura, Emma and Lucy about, if she wanted to. But maybe she wouldn't tell anyone, maybe she would just treasure it. Of course she might let a little bit slip every now and then. At the thought of their faces she smiled a long slow smile. It had been a good holiday after all, one of the very best.